THE
SEVENTH
REFLECTION

THE SEVENTH REFLECTION

MYRON CURTIS

iUniverse, Inc.
Bloomington

THE SEVENTH REFLECTION

iUniverse books may be ordered through booksellers or by contacting:

iUniverse
1663 Liberty Drive
Bloomington, IN 47403
www.iuniverse.com
1-800-Authors (1-800-288-4677)

ISBN: 978-1-4759-9287-8 (sc)
ISBN: 978-1-4759-9288-5 (ebk)

Library of Congress Control Number: 2013909656

Printed in the United States of America

iUniverse rev. date: 06/03/2013

I

Laurenz Kapro took off his white lab coat, hung it in the closet, and donned his jacket. He retrieved the light muffler from a side pocket and placed it around his neck, as the autumn air of New York had acquired some bite. Taking a few steps toward the door, he turned and surveyed the lab. Generators for electromagnetic fields and localized space warps, lasers, dark matter simulators, and Schrodinger chambers cluttered the room in a disordered array.

All that equipment . . . looks like a pile of junk, thought Laurenz. *The least satisfying way to do science—the Mr. Magoo approach. Of course, the clutter represents years of work we built up piece by piece, each stage inspired by the results before. There is certainly nothing neat about it, which belies the myth of orderly progress from concept to conclusion, first on paper then in the lab with real results. Maybe the idea of parallel worlds is a myth like many . . . what the hell, most of my peers keep saying.*

He was the last of the bare-bones staff to leave, and it fell to him to make sure all was properly shut down to prevent damage to the equipment. He turned to go.

All lights out and everything is powered down. Don't think I missed anything, no . . . there. What's that?

In the dark, a glow was emanating from one of the chambers. Something was on.

It's probably just a work light, hardly worth weaving through that tangle of apparatus to extinguish.

He sighed, took a breath, and threaded his way through the obstacle course of devices and improvised wiring. Reaching the chamber, he paused. Light emanated from one of the devices involved in the entanglement experiments. It was not the warm glow of incandescence, but of an eerie, blue-green variety. Laurenz peered inside. Seemingly projected against the dark interior was a glow—the source of the illumination. It took a minute for his eyes to focus. He stared at the thing—three intersecting lines forming a triangle. He angled himself square on, to the screen.

It appears to have one right angle and is not projected from any place as it seemed at first, thought Laurenz. He looked around on the chance that it may have emanated from some other source. He looked back. *It's just there, suspended in the spatial interior of the chamber without any hint of its origin.*

Standing mesmerized for a moment, Laurenz pulled himself together, stumbled back to the lab office, and grabbed a camera. He hurried back to the chamber and quickly took several photos of the strange apparition with a sense that some hidden message might be buried in the image. He remained for what must have been a half hour when, in a blink, the image was gone.

He was sweating, even in the chill of the lab whose heat always was turned off on the assumption that no one could possibly be there after bankers' hours. Grabbing his cell phone, he called Nate Brock, his colleague and stalwart comrade in defense of the project.

"Here," responded a sleepy Nate. "I was just taking a short nap before going out."

"I think we have an indication," said Laurenz, striving for calm.

"What!" Nate said, instantly coming alive.

"It's no little green man holding forth—only a geometric form, a triangle suspended eerily in one of the space-warp chambers. I took photos until it finally disappeared."

"I'll be right over," said Nate.

A half hour later the two were poring over the photos, which Laurenz had uploaded to his computer and printed out.

"It was just a triangle," said Laurenz. "But there it was, hanging there like a mobile with no wires. Here, take a look at this one. I tried to get perpendicular to the plane of the triangle."

"Okay," said Nate. "That's a right-angled triangle all right. Let's see if there's something special about it like the ones they put in those space capsules. Where's a ruler?" He rummaged through drawers as he mumbled to himself. "You'd think that with all the junk around here to deal with numbers, a simple ruler might be had."

"I'll get one from the janitor's tool box," said Laurenz, laughing as he moved to a nearby closet and rummaged around. Returning to the board where the prints were scattered about, he passed the ruler to Nate, who had chosen one which appeared to be a straight-on view, perpendicular to the plane of the triangle.

"Now," said Laurenz as he measured the sides, "write this down. The short one is . . . 14.3 centimeters as near as I can measure, and the long one is . . . nineteen, more or less. What's that ratio?"

"Point seven five, or close to it," said Nate.

"Well I'll be damned," said Laurenz. "That's three-to-four, and look at the shape of that thing. It's a three-four-five, right-angled triangle whatever their unit of measure—no doubt about it and no accident. The triangle alone would suggest intelligence, but perhaps our senders thought that the three intersecting lines might be viewed as merely a phenomenon born of happenstance, so they jazzed it up as a three-four-five. Somebody at minimum is trying to say: 'I am here and have some degree of cognitive skill.' The question is where is 'here,' and how do we go forward? As of now, there is no way to reciprocate. Can you stick around and keep an eye on it? I'm bushed and emotionally drained from the contact—or whatever it is. I was supposed to meet Marcia, and I am late. She will be pissed."

"I will stay for a while to see if anything else comes through," said Nate.

Laurenz charged out of the lab to the student center where he found Marcia waiting. His other colleague, Sye Mallert, waved as he entered. Marcia didn't seem particularly upset that Laurenz had not called but was clearly expecting some sort of explanation.

"I am sorry. I ran into something at the lab that had to be attended to," said Laurenz.

"What could possibly be more important than your date with me?" said Marcia with feigned gravity as she brushed her coal black hair from a dazzlingly beautiful face.

"Actually, nothing . . . well, my research competes neck and neck with my affection for you."

"What?!" said Marcia, still with a mode of mock indignation.

"Marcia, when are you going back to Rio?" asked Laurenz, changing the subject.

"During spring break, which is upon us; just after exams; and then again after graduation in the summer, which, of course, is winter there," said Marcia. "Of immediate concern is my father, who just had an operation. Going to miss me?"

"That's for sure," said Laurenz. "You are the only thing that keeps me from going bonkers, seeing we are stuck in a holding pattern at the lab."

"What do you mean stuck?" said Marcia. "I thought experimental science just chugged along, each day adding a little more data."

"Usually it does, but we are cutting-edge, working on something that is way out there and, frankly, looked on with derision by our scientific colleagues. As I have told you, Nate, Sye, and I have been going it alone with little support, financial or otherwise. If it were not for the United Mystics Coalition, we would be fundless. It is a bit galling that we have to depend on that den of crackpots to do serious science. We all know they are in it for its occult aspect. But frankly, if—"

"Oh, I meant to tell you," interrupted Sye, picking up on Laurenz' remark from his table nearby. "We got a call from Ms. Freeland of the UMC."

"As I was saying," said Laurenz, momentarily distracted. "If our aim is ever realized, it will be regarded as metaphysical by almost everyone outside the circle of hard-nosed scientists. And perhaps we will be so transfixed by the reality of it that we will come over to their point of view, since any consideration of other dimensions or its corollary—parallel worlds—takes us away from classical physics into a misty Valhalla. We have skidded down that slippery slope ever since we were afflicted with Heisenberg and his uncertainty principle and Schrodinger with his damn cat."

"What did she want?" asked Laurenz, belatedly focusing on Sye's comment.

"Who?" said Sye, already distracted by the lapse in the exchange.

"Freda, Freda Freeland, executive VP over there at the UMC—you know she calls the shots there. They must want something to show for their money."

"She would like to come down for a progress report on the project," said Sye.

"Figures. We will have to settle on something to tell her to keep her revved up, but mainly we need for her to keep her mouth shut about what is going on here. The more publicity we get, the more radical and kooky it is going to seem, and the university might step in and disown us."

"Freda aside," said Marcia, "you have lost me on the project. Is it that far out? I can follow the general idea of what you are trying to do, but just where are you stuck, if you can explain it to me in simple language."

"Well, in the simplest terms, to prove the existence of a parallel universe, we must make contact with it," said

Laurenz. "I don't mean someone to just say 'howdy.' It could be anything—any indication sent by a sentient being to demonstrate intelligence. We don't know if there are none, one, or an infinite number of these parallel universes, or, if there is, whether there is likely to be any entity within it to respond. We could be alone, as all religions imply and even some scientists conclude. But coincidentally, there has been a bizarre and unexplainable occurrence that gives us a clue. It is the reason I was late. It came in the form of a geometrical image that appeared in one of the chambers at the lab. Nate and I think it indicates some contact—that is, a response to our efforts—but it could be just an artifact of some lab process."

"What do you think this 'it' would be if you made contact with it?" asked Marcia.

"Like I said, we don't know, but we feel that some . . . something is trying to reach us."

"That's enough for one sitting," said Marcia. "Not that I am diminishing the grandeur of your quest, I just don't have the background to fully appreciate it."

"I apologize. I am taking it out on anybody who will listen to my frustrations," said Laurenz. "I am depressed that you will be gone even for a few days. Perhaps I could come down to Rio in a few days, especially after the issue of this maybe contact is resolved one way or another."

"That might work," said Marcia, picking up the idea. "I must first see my father through the current health crisis and indulge the family rituals, and if we time it right, we could be together for a few days before I have to return to school."

"Let's plan on it then," said Laurenz. "For now, let's get a bite to eat. I can savor your presence and forget about the problems at the lab."

"I'm definitely for that," said Marcia. "I could use some solid food for a change. My schedule is so tight at mealtimes and only allows some quick snacks at the student cafeteria."

"If you are in for Italian, we can go over to Mario's," said Laurenz.

"Sounds good," said Marcia.

They were finishing up at the restaurant when Laurenz' cell rang.

"Yeah."

It was Nate. "We have another indication."

"What is it this time?" said Laurenz.

"Same triangle," said Nate. "I photographed it, and it checked out as a three-four-five, like the first one."

"That's great. It eliminates the possibility of some aberration in the equipment, and it appears we may be on to something at last. Why don't you wrap it up there and get some rest. We can continue tomorrow," said a jubilant Laurenz as he disconnected.

"Sorry about that," said Laurenz. "Nate stayed on at the lab to see if anything else was going to happen." He glanced at his watch, which indicated 10:12 p.m. *Six hours more or less since the first sign*, he thought.

"What was it?" said Marcia in polite response.

"It was the—let's not talk shop. Unless you have to get back to the dorm, I thought we could take a romantic stroll along the lake."

"Curfew is at twelve, so we will have to make it quick," said Marcia. "Next year if I go to grad school, I'm going for private housing."

They just made it back to the dorm in time. Laurenz gave her a quick peck on the lips and melted at her parting smile.

II

Laurenz arrived early at the lab still a little groggy from the excitement of yesterday. The light emanating from the chamber jarred him out of his funk. The path to the chamber was now clear. Nate had cleared away the maze of wires and equipment. Rushing to the spot, Laurenz saw another specter-like image suspended in the chamber.

"It's a . . . a pentagon," mumbled Laurenz. He gazed at it for a long moment. *Equal sides, a regular pentagon, and not surprising . . . no message within the form—only the form itself—but it is enough to reinforce the idea that some entity with intelligence is striving for contact.*

He went for the camera. By the time Nate and Sye arrived at the lab, the image had disappeared.

"It was there when I arrived and disappeared not too long after," said Laurenz. "It's been around ten hours since the image of the triangle appeared, unless there was another during the night when we weren't here. Now, if the interval between the first appearance of the triangle and the second that you saw around six hours later has any meaning, the pentagon or whatever should reappear around noon."

They waited anxiously through the morning; suddenly, at 11:47 a.m., the pentagon reappeared only to disappear after the expected interval of around a half hour.

"I don't suppose we could hope that something new will now appear after another ten-hour interval," said Sye, who, though not privy to the first sighting, had joined in the excitement.

The three spent a restless afternoon tinkering with the equipment and indulging in small talk while the ten-hour interval ticked away. At approximately 10:05 p.m., another geometric figure appeared, only this time it was neatly framed in a rectangle with the long sides on the vertical.

"I wonder what that means," said Sye.

"Another regular polygon, this time of one, two . . . seven sides and incased in a rectangle," said Laurenz, ticking off the sides with his finger. "Yes, that rectangle around it must mean something. It's late, and we all need some rest. Set up the camera to monitor the chamber, and we will see if the thing repeats itself at around four o'clock and accords to the six-hour cycle. If so, we will be here tomorrow after the next ten-hour interval to see if a new image comes through."

They all scattered to their quarters or delayed obligations. Laurenz took a chance and called Marcia. "I hope it is not too late," he said when she answered the phone.

"Not by a long shot," said Marcia. "I'm cramming for finals just before spring break. I haven't heard from you all day but figured the lab has kept you geeks completely occupied."

"Yes it has," replied Laurenz seriously, ignoring the jab. "Two other images have appeared at predictable intervals, more strongly indicating contact and in some weird way, urgency. By the way, you are the only one outside our small circle who knows about this? I would ask you to not mention it to anyone. If the military got wind of it, they would classify it, mainstream research might co-op the project leaving us on the sidelines, and the weirdoes who sponsor us would blab all over the place to exploit the voodoo aspects of it."

"My lips are sealed," said Marcia, a bit excited that she was in on something she didn't fully understand but sensed was of importance.

"Will I see you before you go?" said Laurenz.

"Maybe for a quickie. I am leaving day after tomorrow in the evening. My last term final is the morning that same day."

"Okay. I'll drive you to the airport, and we can solidify my plans to come down to Rio then," said Laurenz.

Another day brought the trio to the lab early. During the night, the heptagon had repeated itself on schedule, and they anxiously awaited the next image. It came later in the day in the form of what appeared to be a crude circle, again framed in a rectangle. They studied the photographs.

"For lack of definition, it looks round, but it's probably another polygon," said Nate.

"I think you are right," said Laurenz,

Sye was already ticking off the short, linear segments that defined the form. ". . . eight, nine, ten, eleven. Eleven sides."

"We already know they are sentient and have some intelligence," said Laurenz. "Maybe they want to underscore it and project a level of sophistication. So, what do we have, polygons of three, five, seven, and eleven sides?"

"Primes!" said Nate almost shouting. "The next one should be thirteen, but if so, it will be hard to count the sides due to the lack of definition in the image."

"Yeah, primes all right, but does it mean anything other than to just reemphasize their intelligence?" asked Laurenz. "And how about that frame around the heptagon? None of the others had it. In any case, the latest indication should repeat again after we are gone. We will wait for the thirteen-sided one sometime tomorrow."

Laurenz was on his way to the airport with Marcia when Nate called to say that the eleven-sided undecagon had indeed repeated itself as expected.

"We will all be there tomorrow when the thirteen-sided one comes in if at all," said Laurenz responding to Nate's update. "They may not send it, believing that they have already made their point."

He disconnected from Nate and said to Marcia, "Things are getting hot back at the lab. Since I talked to you, we have had three more indications, each in the form of a polygon—you know, a closed thing with sides. We have predicted what the next one will be."

"I know what a polygon is," said Marcia. "I got an A in high school geometry. Just because I am in the humanities doesn't mean I don't know anything else."

"I wasn't trying to talk down to you," said Laurenz. "It's just a habit. Most of the things we deal with in the lab are abstruse and arcane. We often strain to explain them in simple terms. I had Sye and Nate in stitches when I was trying to sell the project to the United Mystics Coalition using language and analogies from *Star Trek* and *Alice in Wonderland*."

Laurenz bid farewell to Marcia and hurried back to the lab. The thirteen-sided figure did come in and repeat some six hours later. With trepidation, they waited for the next image figure in fear that due to lack of definition in the image, seventeen sides could not be precisely determined. After the ten-hour interval, to the surprise and relief of all, it was not the seventeen-sided figure expected, indicating the next in the succession of primes. Once again, they were confronted with the heptagon encased in the luminous frame. They waited the requisite interval, and again the unexpected happened. This time only a series of concentric rectangles minus the heptagon appeared as a series of repeating images, each slightly diminished in size.

The three sat around the cluttered workbench in a collective thumb-twiddle with photos of the final image spread out before them.

"I count seven images, as perhaps suggested by the heptagon. Are they pushing the number seven? Any ideas?" asked Laurenz. "They made their point with the polygons and have reverted to another image suggesting the same thing."

"Not a clue," said Nate squinting, adding frivolously, "it looks almost like what you'd see in if you put two mirrors facing each other."

"Right," said Laurenz, picking up Nate's airy mood, "eerily so."

Laurenz broke the long silence that followed.

"Nate, you may have just hit on it. That last image—the reiteration of the rectangle—struck a bell, but I just couldn't place it. Beyond that, what do we know? First of all, they know we are here. Then they tell us, at least, that they can count, they understand Euclidian geometry, and they recognize the special status of prime numbers. It is intended to tell us something but what?"

"Well, in addition to the heptagon, there were the seven repetitions of the image in the last transmission," said Sye. "They are pushing the number seven? Maybe it is a tip on a horse in the seventh at Belmont."

"Good a guess as any," said Laurenz, laughing.

"Along with the images, we can't forget the important fact that they can transmit it to us in some way, which implies some sort of advanced technology," said Nate.

"Right," said Laurenz. "The primitive nature of the contact might suggest that they are either limited in their capacity to communicate or are assuming the minimum with regard to our capabilities of detecting much less understanding the transmissions. They seem to be telling us to concentrate on the last image, the series of rectangles. What the hell does that say?"

"And there is another question," said Sye. "For this primitive contact, did they respond to our inter-dimensional probing, and if so, which of our countless efforts sparked a reply?"

"My guess is that a change of conditions, even an error, in one of our entanglement experiments inadvertently pierced the barrier separating us from this alternate world, and we just stumbled into contact with it," said Laurenz.

"A power drop could have sent things askew," said Sye.

"Yeah, or a surge," said Nate. "Whatever it was, it is useless if we can't duplicate it."

"Let's let it rest, and we can take it up again tomorrow," said Laurenz. "I am thinking that we can take the electronic log, cut out that chamber, and search for anomalies in the data components. For now, I'm bushed, as I'm sure you are. Oh—I promised Marcia that I would come down to Rio for a few days. I don't have to leave till day after tomorrow, so I will be around for another day to see if we can come up with something."

Two days of scrutinizing the data did not shed any light on the mysterious appearance of the succession of images.

"There are variations in the data readout but similar variations are found in all the chambers," said Nate. "Whatever it was that delivered the breakthrough was below our threshold of detection."

"Looks like we are stuck for now," said Laurenz. "I am leaving later today. You guys continue the schedule till I get back. If you come up with anything, call me."

III

Laurenz boarded the plane preoccupied and brooding. He picked at the meal offering and mulled over the project as he sipped on the double scotch he had paid extra for. Drowsiness overcame him, and he faded into the night to the drone of the jet engines. He woke to the sound of the intercom and light streaming through the windows. The modest breakfast brought him to some semblance of alertness. Wading through the sea of hawkers who plagued unsuspecting tourists, he grabbed a cab.

"Hotel Gloria por favor," said Laurenz, evoking his limp Portuguese.

The driver responded with the universal "okay."

Laurenz arrived somewhat tired and scruffy and settled in his room at the Gloria. *That trip always flattens me,* he thought. *I need a shower, a shave, and some real breakfast to recover.*

He stepped into the shower. The warm water cascaded over the uneven contours of his body, reviving and bringing him to full alertness. The thought kept coming back. *After a shave, I can call Marcia.* Stepping in front of the bathroom mirror covering the door of the medicine cabinet, he took stock of himself. There was at least eighteen hours of beard there. He looked away momentarily and looked back, for the first time noticing the peculiar effect made by the mirror mounted on the door behind in opposition to the cabinet mirror. Because the two mirrors were not precisely parallel to each other, he saw himself as a series of repeating images. *One Laurenz Kapro is enough,* he thought jovially as still another thought lingered just below the surface. He stood gazing at the image, the moments passing

Erie, thought Laurenz. *It resembles the final image from the contact—the same image repeated, overlapping, and diminishing in size. Could this really have anything to do with what came through at the lab? Not likely but still a weird coincidence,* Laurenz told himself.

He gazed down the image series, which due to the sparse illumination in the room and the small size of the mirrors, dwindled quickly to darkness while curving off to the side. After four or five back and forth "bounces," his own image, in alternating reflections showing front and back, was nearly invisible. What was visible, however, was a fuzzy specter, glowing faintly, and embedded somewhere in the reflected series after several of the bounces.

Now that's odd.

He finished shaving and immediately called Marcia. "Hi, it's me. When can I see you?"

"I'm dying to see you, but this evening is bad for now," said Marcia. "I may have empty spots during the day, though, and I have plans for you to come over here to meet the family. I live over in Gavea on the fringe of the city, in the shadow of the statue of Christ the Savior on Mount Corcovado. It would take me at least half an hour to get to the Gloria."

"Yes, I know more or less where that is from my previous visits here before I met you," said Laurenz. "I'll call—no, you call me here at the Gloria when you are settled and have your schedule sorted out. I have a couple of things to look into here relating to the work back at the lab."

"I can't imagine what that could be, but have your fun," said Marcia.

She didn't call. Laurenz was disappointed but not surprised. Her family was close-knit and rallied in the face of tragedy or setback. In this case, it was the health of Fernando, patriarch of the Amaral clan.

Laurenz went down to the pool and sat musing. A gnawing thought kept intruding. *Uncanny as it seems, there would seem to be an eerie connection between that reflection phenomena in the bathroom mirror and the contact at the lab. If there is, it is not location specific. Here I am—thousands of miles from the first experience of it, and it intrudes again. Assuming the connection, why am only I the only one aware of it? Besides its obscure nature, it is probably because I am the only one looking for it, but how can I possibly test it? One thing is sure, if mirrors are the key, it would require better illumination, higher fidelity in the mirrors themselves, and a larger size. I guess we could rig up something at the lab. Till then, I will have to sit on it.*

He took a dip in the pool, dried off, and sat for a moment as it came to him. *Colombo. Confeitaria Colombo, the dominating decorative feature there is the array of huge mirrors lining the walls of the dining salon. This is completely unknown territory. I can at least give it a try and see how far it goes.*

Laurenz hated dining alone. Being alone, it would be easy for him to pick up a Brazilian beauty, but he was committed, and Marcia was proud and possessive. Hotel Gloria was not far from the center of the city, *Centro* by local designation, where *Colombo* was located. Evening arrived, and Laurenz exited the hotel and made his way past the landscaped park areas adjacent to the main ways leading to *Centro*, across the public gardens to *Rua Gonçalves Dias*, a modest side street running parallel to *Avenida Rio Branco, Centro's* main drag. Colombo loomed just ahead amid a jumble of shops and street-side eateries that were in the process of closing. He entered and was seated in the great salon of the *Confeitaria.*

His thoughts drifted as he waited for service. *Maybe I shouldn't have come to Rio at all. Marcia will be locked into familial duties.* With a sigh, his thoughts drifted back to the project. *The whisper of a response we got through the chamber in the Parallel World Communicator bank was encouraging, but where will it lead? Parallel world one is there somewhere. Even if a link can be made to communicate, other than the primitive symbols, can it be understood?*

A polite voice broke his reverie, "Would you like to order, sir?"

"Uh—yes."

Laurenz chose from the night's offerings and requested a cocktail while he waited.

The fabulous interior of Colombo always held him in a kind of captive state. The dominating feature overwhelming the interior was the series of giant mirrors lining the sides of the salon. Each was mounted in an ornate frame decorated in the Portuguese colonial style. But it was not so much the mirrors themselves that dominated the scene; it was their interaction with one another, whether intended or inadvertent. Placed in approximate opposition, they showed a continuous repeating reflection of the view of the interior of the restaurant. This, in theory, went on to infinity but in practice dwindled to a murky blur after several reflections, since each bounce increased, by the width of the room, the distance from which the original scene was viewed. As a consequence, the size of the reflected image itself and all details within it were correspondingly diminished by the law of inverse squares, with the original reflected scene gradually moving to one side out of sight because of the minute aberration in their parallel alignment. Adding to the effect was a subtle darkening of each successive reflection due to the fact that the mirrors themselves could not perform with 100 percent efficiency in reflecting the scene.

Laurenz sipped his cocktail and carefully scrutinized the mirrors. The image in the first mirror showed him sitting in contemplation and those around him at orderly arranged tables engaged in a random conversation. His attention moved to the second reflection, which showed him and fellow diners viewed from the back, all slightly diminished in size. His focus was shifting to the third reflection but was interrupted.

"Excuse me," said the waiter as he brought the selections ordered, jolting Laurenz from his preoccupation with the mirrors.

"Thank you," said Laurenz.

He concentrated on the food and monitored some of the conversation at the adjoining tables, most of it in Portuguese but with a sprinkling of English mixed in. As he waited for dessert, his attention again returned to the mirrors. There he was with a scowl on his face embedded in the busy scene, the scowl and the scene as a whole becoming smaller and less distinct as he scanned the successive images. Captured by the novelty of it, he considered. *The effect of placing mirrors in opposition to one and other is familiar to everyone, but as manifested in such a grand scale at Colombo, it takes on an eerie, otherworldly character.*

He casually scanned the next reflection, and the next, each less defined than its predecessor until—there it was. There, in the seventh reflection, was something—something that was not here. The frame at that level was dimmed to a fraction of its original intensity and vaguely showed a part of the original scene but also something more. He slowly turned to make sure the anomaly did not originate in the scene around him, realizing immediately that checking didn't make any sense. If it was not present in preceding reflections one through six, it should not be present in the seventh.

Apparently no one else notices it, he thought. *It's not surprising. In the visual chaos of repeating images, each repeating the cacophony of activity in the salon, any detail is not likely to be scrutinized.*

He pondered while squinting at the blurred outline. *Is it a face? Yes, perhaps a face of sorts in its most basic form, flat and expressionless. In any case, it is a partial resolution, an upgrade of the faint luminous dot he saw in the bathroom mirror.*

The waiter interrupted with the dessert, once again jolting Laurenz from his pondering stupor. "Would you like some coffee?"

"Yes, some espresso please," said Laurenz in a distracted daze.

He finished the dessert and slowly sipped the coffee all the while staring at the image in the seventh reflection. Suddenly, the anomaly was no longer there, which was a relief, because he was beginning to think he might just be seeing things. He lingered for a time but concluded the image would not return.

Laurenz called for the check and left the restaurant somewhat light-headed. It was too much to digest in so short a time. He decided it was such a beautiful night that he would walk back to the Gloria, retracing his steps back down the Rua Gonzales Dias. The gardens were a little spooky at this hour, so he walked down the short stint along their border, back onto the now sparsely inhabited right of ways flanking the main traffic arteries. These were lit, but with patches of dimness and shadow. He was scarcely aware of the footsteps behind as he was fallen upon by several unknown ruffians. Had it been one or two, he could have easily held his own, bringing to bear his skills in self-defense. But the tangle of arms and bodies that enveloped him was too much. They took just about everything he had on him, but aside from some scrapes and bumps in the scuffle, they did him little harm. His assailants faded into the amorphous sponge of the Rio night, disappearing into the innumerable pathways radiating from the scene. He struggled back to the hotel and called Marcia.

"It's late. What is it?" said Marcia.

"I went out to eat, and coming back I got mugged."

"Are you all right?" she asked with apprehension.

"Yes, they took my watch and what I had on me, but fortunately my passport, extra credit card, and cash were in the box at the hotel, and the watch was a cheap one."

"Where were you?"

"In that sort of no man's land coming back from Colombo to the Gloria."

"So you are okay? You must be careful here in Rio. Were you there alone?"

"When I got mugged?"

"No, you dolt, at Colombo."

"No, there were lots of people," teased Laurenz, sensing that Marcia might be just a little jealous.

"That's not what I mean," pouted Marcia.

"Yes, I was alone. You know you are the only one," said Laurenz. "But something did happen there—at Colombo, that is—something weird that I have to share with someone."

"What weird thing could possibly happen at Colombo?"

"It has to do with what I told you earlier about the work at the lab, something about the mirrors," said Laurenz with hesitation.

"I'll humor you on this," said Marcia after a pause. "Colombo is not the lab. Perhaps you are hallucinating. Can you tell me more about it?"

"Possibly so, but I have to trust my senses and sanity," said Laurenz. "What I saw doesn't lend itself very well to verbal explanation. Maybe if we have dinner there, I can show you firsthand. Then again, maybe not, because the thing—the effect—vanished after an interval."

"I haven't the foggiest idea what you are talking about. Let's see . . . yes. I'm free tomorrow night. Now, no walking around Rio after dark. I'll stop by in a taxi around eight."

"Okay, see you then."

Laurenz sighed and hung up. The day had been a drag until he went to Colombo. The vision, for want of a better word, had jarred him out of the funk that had consumed him, and the jostling he received in the mugging left him with a surge of adrenaline that had yet to subside. He showered and slipped into bed, but he could not sleep. His mind kept returning to the project

I am displaced from the lab by at least six thousand miles, the only place there was any inkling of contact with another world, but I could be sitting on Mars for all the difference it would make. I always suspected that like the spooky action of quantum entanglement, any distance short of the infinite is irrelevant. That apparition I saw or thought I saw at Colombo, it made little sense trying to connect the experience with the work at the lab, but that was the first thing that popped into my mind. What do the two things have in common? Both defied reality, both appeared as suspended in midair, and . . . both occurred in my presence.

I—the *Chosen One,* Laurenz mused melodramatically with a subdued chuckle. *Or am I?*

Sobering thoughts welled up in him. *The figures that appeared in the lab are a response to activity that originated there. In contrast, at least in theory, the image at Colombo will appear anyplace there are mirrors large enough to display repeated reflections with adequate fidelity, but in practice, the Colombo setting is unique because of the mirrors themselves. In the absence of motivation, commercial, esthetic, or scientific reasons, mirrors on such a grand scale would not be produced or juxtaposed in such a unique way in another setting. This means that accidental discovery of the figure in the mirror was unlikely. Good. I can imagine a mass freak out.*

Soon sleep clouded and then overcame his silent musings.

IV

Light streamed through the window. Laurenz awoke to the sounds of children frolicking in the pool just outside and below. The sleep had cleared his mind.

I am now certain that the indications we have by chance stumbled upon may be only two of a multitude of unrecognized efforts by another dimension to gain contact, so we best concentrate on them, he thought. *Assuming the Colombo image will reappear; can I resolve it and make it clear? I might be able to see it more clearly with some optical aid, but I can't just go there tonight with a pair of binoculars. At best, I would look like some weirdo, distract the other diners, and embarrass Marcia. At worst, I would be carted off as disturbed. I have to get closer. A monocular—I can put it up to my eye using one hand. If I don't overdo it, linger only briefly, and weather Marcia's sarcasm, it may not be noticed.*

Laurenz searched for a local shop that might have anything like a monocular and finally found a used one in the district around *Av. Mem de Sa´*, a commercial street with just about everything in hardware, new and used. He passed the day taking in some of the tourist attractions that Rio had to offer but could not resist the temptation to drop into Colombo for a brief lunch. A quick look at the reflections revealed no image, no abnormality of any kind. Somewhat disappointed, he retired to the Gloria and relaxed at the pool.

I hope I have better luck tonight, thought Laurenz. *If not, Marcia will surely think I have flipped.*

Evening finally arrived, and at length Marcia showed up at the Gloria.

A half hour late, noted Laurenz. *Brazilians are not known for their punctuality.* They hailed a taxi and headed for Colombo. The maître d' lead them to a secluded table to the side of the salon.

This won't do, thought Laurenz. *From here, the reflection shows only part of the original scene. It's chopped off by the mirror adjacent to it. I was lucky the first time being centered on one of the mirrors; otherwise, I would not have been able to see that image in the seventh reflection.*

If you don't mind, could we sit at that table over there?" Laurenz inquired anxiously.

The maître d shrugged and ushered them over to the new location, while Laurenz didn't miss Marcia's raised eyebrow.

"Thank you so much," said Laurenz as they were seated.

"Fussy, fussy. What was that all about?" whispered Marcia.

"What I hope to show you can't be seen from this vantage point. We have to be square on to these mirrors. Just a second while I give a quick look." Laurenz scanned the reflections for the telltale glow that set the image apart from the repeating scenes. "No, not there. I was a little later last night, and if the 'thing' has a schedule, we are early. Let's order a cocktail—no, wait. Can you drink in Brazil at twenty?"

"No problem here," said Marcia. "The MDA is eighteen, and even that is lightly enforced."

Laurenz sipped his straight-up scotch, and Marcia dawdled over a simple martini. They ordered from the night's offerings and settled into the intimacy so long delayed.

"So, how go the family matters, and when will I get a chance to meet the clan?" Laurenz asked.

"I've been thinking about having you over for dinner on Saturday," said Marcia. "You can't imagine how uncasual such a get-together can be. Everyone will assume this and that and ask leading questions. I expect you to be on your best behavior . . . and maybe it would be best not to mention the specifics of your work. My family is very straight-laced, and your activities are suggestive of the supernatural and occult. If asked, ply them with some benign generalities."

"I see what you mean. You would be interested to know that I avoid the subject with my dad for the same reasons."

The waiter brought their order, and they settled down to quiet, intimate dining. In the warmth of the moment, Laurenz had almost forgotten his main reason for being there. Amid the flow of small talk, he glanced and absentmindedly scanned the reflections.

There it is.

Marcia immediately noticed the stillness that enveloped him. "What is it?" she said quietly.

"It's there," said Laurenz, answering in kind and unmoving as if doing so would cause the image to disappear.

"Can I see it?"

"Yes, as a matter of fact, I would be glad for someone to assure me that I am not imagining the whole thing. Because of the nature of the phenomenon, rather than asking you to swivel and face the same mirror I am facing, I would first ask you to look in the mirror you are now facing and count the frames to the seventh one."

Marcia cocked her head to the left and slightly upward and focused on the reflections. For a moment she seemed to be counting off the frames. Suddenly, she said in a whisper, "Yes, I do see it. It is as you said, fuzzy and indistinct with a slight glow around it, but there is definitely something there. What on earth does it mean?"

"In general, it may mean that as a result of our probing, they have evidence that we are here, there is a parallel world, and they have found a way to contact us," said Laurenz. "As an overture, they first sent us the primitive symbols we stumbled on at the lab. They were to suggest a way forward and did by representing pictorially the repeated images like those we see here. In short, they have found some way to use the mirrors as a medium for contact. Now that I have found out what they were getting at, we can move to that next step. Who knows how many other efforts may have been employed that went unnoticed. Moreover, since you see it in the opposite direction, it is not direction or location specific, which suggests that any similar configuration of mirrors will show the image."

"Can you respond in some way?" asked Marcia.

"The trouble is . . . Well, the trouble is that this latest contact, if that's what it is, makes no sense from the standpoint of either science or common sense. The reflection of a mirror is merely the response of a reflecting surface to a scene illuminated by radiation—in this case, visible light. That thing up there is not in the original scene. Somehow in the succession of bounces, they have managed to insert something. It is so bizarre that I have hesitated to call Nate and Sye about it."

Marcia was quiet for a moment. She glanced again at the image. "That could be a picture of something rather than something."

"You are undoubtedly right," said Laurenz.

"Can't you in some way put an image of yourself there in the seventh reflection in some form, an image or . . . maybe, your actual self to say hi?" she said, her voice rising gleefully at the end.

Laurenz' mouth twitched as he stared off in space. The thing had not moved or shown any signs of life or animation.

Without moving, he focused on Marcia. "Maybe," he said with increasing respect for the object of his affections, "just maybe we could do something like that. Of course, to be of any use in communicating, we would have to send a functioning analog of myself, not just a static image. It would also be useless unless the image there has similar capabilities, and the encounter was confined to the . . . the enclosure, for want of a better word, of the seventh reflection. But back to what we actually see—that fuzzy specter. I had hoped to discreetly resolve the image into something more definite, so I brought along this instrument," said Laurenz, taking the monocular from his pocket. "It's primitive, but I dared not bring anything more conspicuous. Using it, I had hoped to discreetly resolve the image into something more definite. I think the patrons who notice will think I bought a new plaything and will ignore it."

Marcia glanced at the monocular. "All right, give it a try, but if you stay at it too long, it will attract attention. If it gets too bad, I will disown you," she said only half joking.

Laurenz looked around. The tables were now more or less full, and the salon appeared normal. Discreet bits of nearby chatter could be discerned and that more distant resolved into an ambient drone. He casually put the monocular to his eye and focused on the image. Laurenz gasped in spite of himself. As he panned the monocular across the series to the seventh reflection, what he saw, in addition to the scene in which he was embedded, was not just a face but the face of another himself surrounded by a faint halo. The image had minor differences. The head possessed no hair, perhaps by choice, but a faint stubble of fresh growth could be seen covering the scalp. The facial features asserted themselves strongly, as if its original were enhanced with a modest amount of makeup.

He was jarred out of his trance by a gentle kick from Maria under the table.

"Well?" said Marcia after a pause.

"It's . . . it's . . . well, you look," said Laurenz, handing her the monocular.

"How do you work this thing?"

"It's already focused. Just point it and look," said Laurenz in a choking tone of hoarse reverence.

Marcia was facing the other way, but they had already determined that the image appeared in seventh frame when viewed from either direction. She put the monocular to her eye. "It looks like . . . Laurenz, it looks like you!" she forced a whisper as she put the monocular down. "It's the weirdest thing I have ever seen."

Laurenz was relieved that Marcia had seen it, as he was beginning to question his senses.

They finished dinner in an atmosphere of restrained conversation and intermittent periods of silence.

"Nate Brock here," said Nate responding to his cell.

"Nate, this is Laurenz. My little recreational sojourn to Rio has turned into quite a saga."

"Trouble with the family?" asked Nate.

"No, at least not yet. It has to do with the project."

"Is somebody down there working in the same area? I thought we were the only nuts around," said Nate.

"No, it's not that. I have come upon something that is surely another attempt at contact."

Nate was silent for a moment and then laughingly quipped, "Have you been attending macumba rituals down there? I knew they would beat us to it."

"No," said Laurenz, continuing on a serious note. "All I can tell you without going on for an hour is that I have, by the most remote accident, received an indication here. I haven't discounted the fact that the indication could be from still another parallel universe. For now, I believe because of a possible relationship to the last image we received at the lab, that it is the same world from which we received the succession of images. To find a way to respond, we must try to duplicate the conditions that have enabled me to detect this continuing attempt at communication in a lab environment."

"Does it call for more equipment? We are maxed out on our fund flow now. Anything big will put us in the red, and you know the United Mystics Coalition comes down out of the sky when it comes to control of their funds. All of sudden they became business men."

"I think we can settle it with regard to this latest issue with just a few bucks. Here's what I want you to do: first, see if we can get two large mirrors."

"Mirrors?"

"I'll explain it when I get back. Just do it."

"How large is large?"

"Well, I am thinking around eight by twelve, but six by ten will probably do."

"I fear you are not talking about inches," said Nate

"Right," said Laurenz. "If you can't find anything close, we will take it from there. If no such thing is available, we might be able to improvise and do it on the cheap."

V

Laurenz donned his best Sunday getup for Marcia's Saturday invite—neat but not too formal, because Carioca's tended to dress casually at social events. To his surprise, Marcia appeared on time, and the two of them made for Gavea. She brought one of the family cars this time, and Laurenz marveled at her handy negotiation of the stick shift, now a rarity in passenger cars back in the United States. They threaded their way up through the Botafogo section, down and flanking the northern shore of the Lagoa Rodreguez Freites. With the steep slopes of Mount Corcovado looming to the right, Gavea lay just ahead. There were many fine houses there nestled in the lush foliage of the hills bordering downtown Rio, but occasional glimpses could be had of small, improvised shacks in secluded nooks of the landscape. These housed many of the service personnel needed for the rich homes and served as a stark reminder of the lingering gaps in the social landscape of Brazil.

Marcia pulled up to one of the more luxurious of the villas and voiced a cheerful, "Here we are."

Laurenz felt a little queasy and noticed a lump in his throat as he alighted from the car and strode toward the twin door entrance to the house. As they approached, a well-dressed woman opened the door and awaited the couple.

"That's Mother," whispered Marcia.

Smiling warmly, she greeted Laurenz with correct but accented English.

"Welcome to our home, Mr. Kapro. The *Senhor* is still convalescing from a recent operation and will join us presently. We have all been anxious to meet you. Marcia has told us so much about you and your work."

I hope not too much, thought Laurenz.

"The pleasure is mine, *Senhora,*" said Laurenz.

"In her enthusiasm, I hope Marcia has not revealed any of my many faults," said Laurenz with strained relaxation.

"We all have them," responded the Senhora easily. "Come, let us go inside and meet some of the family."

The lump was still there as they passed through the inner chambers of the house. The entered a broad, lounge-like space, the Brazilian equivalent of a living room, which was casually peopled with several of the clan. Laurenz quickly counted five men, including two of student age, and most important, a distinguished-looking gentleman seated in a wheelchair.

That's the big cheese there, the padrone who will have to pass on me, thought Laurenz.

There were at least five women who greeted them, including the Senhora and one of younger age, Marcia's sister. The conversation ceased as the three approached. Just as the lump started to assert itself again, the Senhora interrupted with multiple introductions, beginning in strict protocol with the Senhor Amaral, patriarch of the clan.

Laurenz acknowledged appropriately each name and at the close choked out a stilted, "It is a pleasure to meet you all. Please continue your conversation in Portuguese," adding as if some enormous burden had been lifted. "From Marcia's influence, I am comfortable with it if not excessively fluent."

Senhor Amaral laughed and said, "You are likely to hear an incomprehensible mixture of both."

Laurenz smiled in response to this easy rejoinder.

Fernando Amaral, he surmised was in his late fifties and seemingly well preserved, but the ashtray of discarded cigarettes, excessive tan, and ample girth betrayed a penchant for old-world habits. Cocktails were served by the servants, and the party settled into small groups with Marcia dragging

Laurenz from one to the other. Marcia's cell rang, and she answered, momentarily leaving Laurenz stranded. The two women in the clump had also been distracted and jabbered away in Portuguese. He wandered into an alcove off the living room that was lined with bookcases and a glass-enclosed case full of small trophies. He strained to read the inscriptions in quasi-gold, but the light was too dim. A voice from behind drew his attention. Laurenz turned to see a handsome young man with dark hair and chiseled features. He stood there relaxed but poised with pent up energy like an athlete at rest.

"I am Marcia's younger brother, Christian," he said, speaking in virtually unaccented English, as he quietly engaged Laurenz in a manner more serious than that set by the occasion. "I am interested in the work you are doing."

The lump in Laurenz' throat that had subsided now returned. He was at pains to present the image of a decorous American working in a stable occupation. He responded with an anemic, "Yes, quantum physics is certainly the field of the future."

"Actually, I meant the particular aspect of it you are in," said Christian.

Laurenz could not immediately come up with some benign response to Christian's latest. To discourage further probing, he opted for a piece of stage business by slowly taking a sip of the drink he was holding. Finally, he dredged up an innocuous, "Well, my group is doing experiments that engage the concept of quantum entanglement."

There was a moment's pause while Christian sipped on his Coke. "What is the United Mystics Coalition?"

Laurenz figured the longer he lingered over a response to Christian's question the more suspicious it would seem. It was obvious that Christian knew more than the rest about his activities. He glanced about. Marcia was still busy on the phone, and the rest of the group had fragmented.

"Where did you hear about them?" said Laurenz casually.

"On the Net," said Christian in a lowered voice. "They came up along with some other stuff about parallel worlds when I googled your name."

Laurenz, struck dumb, was about to respond but was rescued by Christian himself.

"That's way out, really cool," said Christian. "You don't have to tell me. This United Mystics Coalition is one of those cult groups who will put money in anything that appears to promote the metaphysical. They even have chapters here. Your work is cutting-edge and looked on by some as kooky, right?"

Laurenz sighed, but feeling he had a friend among the "enemy," he responded, "You have it right, and I would appreciate you're not blabbing around the—the details of my work. It might seem a bit strange to your family. By the way, where did you learn English so well?"

"Watching movies. Of course, what we have in school forms a basis," said Christian. "And don't worry. Nobody else around here uses a computer for anything except for an occasional e-mail to a relative."

As they turned to go, Laurenz said to Christian, "These trophies, what are they for?"

"Oh, they are mine, relegated to this dark corner by my mother, who has reservations about my sports activity."

"And what is that?"

"Judo. Mother thinks it is too violent. Wants me to play tennis instead," said Christian as they rejoined the others.

The entire company retired to the dining area where at the enormous table Laurenz mercifully was flanked by Marcia and Christian. Fernando, patriarch of the Amaral clan, was seated in his wheelchair at the head of the table. He slowly rose and raised his glass in a toast: "To our American friend."

It seemed to Laurenz that he had passed muster with Fernando and the rest of the family.

The evening wound down, and they were about to take leave when Christian took Laurenz to the side. "I haven't told

Marcia yet, but I have applied to Inland U for a scholarship to study physics. Foreign students sometimes have an advantage in that area. If I don't get it, I will seek acceptance there anyway. I was wondering if you need any help at the lab. Not the heavy stuff, of course, because I am not qualified for it, but there must be a host of pick-and-shovel tasks around that your team has to do because there is nobody else. You know, like those immigrants you keep getting from the south who do the jobs Americans don't want to do. In the process, I could learn something."

Laurenz looked at Christian trying, not to laugh. "You are not trying to bribe me are you?"

"No, definitely not," replied Christian, laughing. "I just think your work is super cool and would like to be a part of it even in a minor way."

"I'll think about it. Look me up if you things work out with regard to your application."

"What are you two up to?" said Marcia, interrupting. "You have been huddled together all evening." With a nod at Christian, she added, "Watch him. He has become disgustingly American."

"We have been discussing Brazilian women," said Christian with a mischievous smirk.

Marcia glared at Laurenz and then back at Christian.

"He has been doing all the talking," said Laurenz, wincing. "And . . . and he brought up the subject. As a matter of fact, I had not even noticed that there were any," he added in a lighter vein.

She ordered, "Get in the car, Laurenz, before you are smitten by a bolt of lightning."

They rode silently back to the Gloria until Laurenz ventured, "Well, how do you think it went?"

"Really well—about like I imagined," said Marcia seriously, her mock indignation in check. "You know you cut a rather dignified figure. They don't know that behind that mask of legitimacy lies a real oddball."

VI

Laurenz checked in on the lab.

"Nate here, I couldn't find mirrors anything like the size you mentioned except some extremely expensive, custom-made ones. Have you thought about making some from scratch?"

"Yes, I suspected what I asked for might not be available, so I had a plan B," said Laurenz. "We can get some large plate glass and make our own. Find out where the mirror manufacturers get it and go from there. We can determine the best way to impart a reflecting surface after they arrive."

"Now, you need to tell me at least something of what this is about," said Nate.

Laurenz sighed. "Actually, I got the hint from you. Remember when you likened the final image to repeated reflections that occur when mirrors are placed in opposition to each other? I was reminded of it when I was shaving in the hotel bathroom, which had mirrors facing one another. Then I noticed an anomaly in the reflections and couldn't figure out what it was because of the poor conditions, but it gave a hint as to a way forward. There is a well-known restaurant in Rio called Colombo, which has large mirrors situated in such a way as a decorative feature, so I went there to see if I could use them to improve on the conditions. The upshot is that the contact seems to have found some way to insert something in the series of reflections, and what they have put in there is an image of me—or at least it looks like me. I'm sure that raises more questions than it answers, and I have a vague sense that it has to do with the initial contact we got in the lab. I will fill in the details when I return. For now, see if you can get the stuff together, so we can test it in the privacy of the lab."

"But—" Nate exploded in a precipitant outburst and then lapsed into silence.

Laurenz picked it up. "I know it doesn't make sense, but it was there, at least the image was, and I was there and saw it. Marcia saw it too. Furthermore, when Marcia saw it, she was viewing it the opposite direction. So it appears that the image is not location specific. I have concluded that if we can reproduce the conditions at Colombo in the lab, we can not only study it in a private setting, but we can ponder some way to respond."

"Okay," said Nate warily. "It appears that we have made a bigger breakthrough than we could have imagined. A world with an alternate 'you' also brings up additional issues: Are there an infinity of these worlds, and if so, why have we made contact with this particular one?"

"We should assume sheer chance until we find out differently," said Laurenz.

"Regarding the glass, I will see if I can get something we can use," said Nate. "To make a useful mirror, it will have to be free of flaws, or we will get some weird, carnival-like effects. When will you be back?"

"Tomorrow," said Laurenz. "I'm taking this evening's flight."

Laurenz went straight from the airport to the lab where Nate and Sye were studying the two large plates. They sat around the workbench and sipped coffee while Laurenz described in more detail his experience at Colombo.

"Did anybody else in the restaurant see it?" asked Sye.

"No," said Laurenz. "It was masked by the clutter and disarray of the scene in general and could only be perceived with careful scrutiny."

A moment of silence ensued while Laurenz' cohorts struggled for some further question of relevance to ask. Finally, Nate ventured, "Exactly where was it?"

"It was always in the seventh reflection," said Laurenz. I know because each time I had to count."

"Seven," exploded Sye as if the thought was solidifying as he spoke. "Another prime and . . . the heptagon, framed in the repeating rectangle."

"I see where you are going," said Nate. "The indication at the lab was a signal. They were telling us that rectangle represented the mirror, and the seven sided heptagon along with the repeated image of both pointed to the seventh reflection."

"Yes," said Laurenz. "They don't know anything about us, like what, if any, language we respond to. The indication they received from us, however, implied some sort of contrived, manmade technology and a basic knowledge of mathematics, hence the symbols. My accidental discovery of the anomaly in the mirror's reflections came from Nate's offhand remark about mirrors facing each other. It is much clearer now that I see it in retrospect.

"Now what we have to do is try to duplicate the conditions at Colombo and improve on them if possible. The best reflecting surface would be the silvering process they use in astronomical telescopes, which would upgrade the reflective efficiency from that at Colombo. But that is a delicate and complicated process, and it would be nearly impossible to make a surface that large chemically clean enough to apply it. We may have to go with a commercial process."

"Then perhaps the easiest path is to use some spray-on silver chemicals and then seal it as they do with the some shellac and paint," said Sye. "Hopefully, the compromise will still retain enough fidelity in the mirrors to let us move ahead."

The team worked feverishly, and after some hitches and redoes, they finally had the mirrors in place. Laurenz moved face on into the mirror as Nate and Sye looked on. He counted the repeated reflections, this time only he himself appeared in the frame, stark compared to the bustling scene at Colombo.

"There are no anomalies," said Laurenz. "There's nothing there in the seventh reflection, but it's early, and if the thing is going to be there, it may be on a schedule. We can start monitoring it around . . . five thirty this evening and should expect it tonight around . . . six o'clock. We are two hours behind Rio at this time of year, and that should be equivalent to the Rio time we saw it."

They waited anxiously through the day into the evening. At the appropriate time, Laurenz said, "Okay, let's give it a try."

He moved into the reflective field and inspected the images. There it was. It now stood out more vividly in the uncluttered setting that now formed the background. Laurenz himself was there, much diminished and slightly to the side of the image. As if afraid to disturb some delicate balance inherent in the spooky phenomena, he quietly motioned Nate and Sye to come to the center of the frame. They both gasped as they viewed the image, which, though vividly described by Laurenz, only hinted at the reality of actually seeing it.

Laurenz broke the spell. "Roll that transit over here and let's take a closer look. It should get us close enough to tell us something about that thing"

Sye wheeled over the transit, which was mounted on casters.

"You guys stand a little to the right. It's better to have the image against a plain background," said Laurenz as he focused and peered through the instrument.

The face—his face—was there. Laurenz heaved a sigh of relief. The idea that the phenomenon was not wedded to any specific location had been a hope, not a certainty.

"Take a look," said Laurenz.

Nate put his eye to the transit. After a quiet moment, he pulled back said, "That thing in there is you all right, minus the hair." He stepped to the side for Sye.

Sye took his turn, lingering at the transit for an extended period.

Then Laurenz took another look and said, "The figure is static with no apparent volition of its own. We can't tell if it is looking back at us or knows we are watching. It seems to be just staring into space. Is there anything we can do to elicit a response?"

"How about a light beam projected through the transit?" said Nate.

"Yeah, or a laser," said Sye.

"The laser is out," said Laurenz. "It might injure its eyes if by chance they react as real ones. We just don't know. Let's try the light. What do we have around here?"

"Well, there's a flashlight in the toolbox," said Nate.

"Hmm . . . too big. It'll have too much wash when we interface it with that small eyepiece in the transit," said Laurenz.

"How about this penlight," said Sye, taking it from his breast pocket.

"Let's see it," said Laurenz, inspecting the light.

Laurenz took the penlight. Making sure the transit was still aimed at the image, he carefully taped the light to the eyepiece of the transit. "Here goes nothing," he said as he gingerly snapped the light on, then off. They had no optical aid now with which to view the image, but Laurenz figured any but the most subtle response could be noted with the naked eye.

There was a collective inhale from the three as they stared intently at the image, which stood immobile for what seemed forever and then suddenly disappeared.

"That was it. Not much but the first real-time, two-way dialog between two worlds, obviously a response to our clumsy probing," said an excited Laurenz. Glancing at his watch, he tentatively concluded that either its time interval lapsed, or they had irritated it. "Let's get some sleep and visit it again tomorrow night."

The next day they drifted through the daily experimental routine preoccupied with the evening's session with the image in the mirror. They broke for an early dinner and returned to the lab.

"I think it's about time," said Laurenz. He slipped into the space between the mirrors and waited.

Nate and Sye hovered on the periphery, waiting for the image to appear. Suddenly, there it was again—the face—right on schedule only this time the image was circumscribed by a ring of light.

"Another signal," said Laurenz. "The thing knows we are here and knows we see it. Now without some common language of communication, we can't go any further. We have to find some way of getting in there, but the problem is so unique that we are starting from scratch. We have to find a new approach. We first have to fathom what we even mean by 'getting in there.' That thing may be a static image, a hologram, or such with enhanced capacities. The response we got was as if it were real. We can start by trying to inject the same in the reflection sequence. Okay . . . any ideas?"

He looked at Nate and Sye, whose blank faces showed that they had not a clue as to how to move forward.

Laurenz heard the hiss of international connection and dull ring.

"*Diga.*"

"Marcia? Marcia darling, I . . . No, I haven't forgotten you," said Laurenz. "We have been so busy at the lab that I haven't had a chance to touch base. We were able to re-create the conditions at Colombo and detect the image you saw. It appears that my suspicions were correct that we can see the image anyplace we create the same conditions.

Anyhow, the thing responded to one of our crude attempts at communication. We are now working on some way to upgrade the quality of the contact.

"So any repercussions from my somewhat shaky visit to your family?" said Laurenz, changing the subject. "I felt all eyes were on me, and I tried to be on my best behavior, but I wasn't sure the king and court were impressed. I felt your younger brother Christian was the only one who had the slightest idea where I was coming from. He had already researched me on the Net, and he thought my way out activity was cool . . . .

"They did? I was afraid I came off as a bumbling idiot. Anyway, that's a relief. And your father—did he say anything? . . .

"That's harmless enough, even gracious, I—

"Christian said what? . . .

"Well, we discussed it, but I don't know if it is a good idea, his working at the lab. We are a tight-knit group. His youthful enthusiasm may not be compatible with our need for secrecy, but I will give him a try. Are you taking the morning flight? . . .

"Okay, I'll meet you at the airport . . . .

"Of course I will have time for you. I will make time."

The day following the response from the object in the mirror, the team plodded through the day's schedule and finally broke early. They decided they would not punish themselves by staying for the scheduled appearance of the image.

"Sye, set up the camera to record the evening's happenings," said Laurenz. "I don't expect anything new."

Nate left the lab. Laurenz was wrapping things up when he glanced over at Sye, who had finished setting up the camera and was staring at the repeated images of himself and the camera.

"Everything okay?" asked Laurenz.

"Uh . . . yeah," said Sye.

"I'm leaving. I have to pick up Marcia. Lock up before you leave."

"Got it," said Sye.

Laurenz picked up Marcia, who was tired from her return flight from Rio, so he took her directly to the dorm. His cell phone went off as he entered his apartment.

"I hope I didn't wake you up." It was Sye.

"No. As a matter of fact, I just got back from the airport. What's up?"

"Well . . . I had an idea. You know I did a stint at the MacDonald Observatory on a student apprentice program during college. They were doing interferometer experiments there, which, as you know, involve the merging of two beams of light. I was wondering if we could somehow harness that basic principal to intrude into the reflection series. I don't know how it would work or what we would project."

"It would have to be a fully functioning analog of one of us," said Laurenz, mulling it over. "It is ridiculous to think we could place anything material in there, but that's an interesting insight and the first hint of a path forward, Sye. Let's sleep on it, and we all can chew it over tomorrow."

The next day the three of them gathered in the lab and waited for inspiration.

"I thought over your suggestion, Sye, and still haven't come up with any way forward," said Laurenz.

"What was that?" asked Nate.

"Well, Sye suggested we use the principle of the interferometer to intrude into the reflection series."

"How would that work?" asked Nate. "A beam of light is a far cry from a material object, much less a thinking person."

"I think we should take the hint from our friends in the other world and settle for something to act for us," said Laurenz.

"That's a quaint way of putting it," said Nate. "I suppose you are talking about some sort of holographic representation. And . . . perhaps it is a little premature, but even if we could accomplish our goal, where would we go from there? Turn it over to the government, who would probably turn it over to the military and classify it? Or would they treat it as another country and send diplomats or even spies?"

"You are right about that," said Laurenz. "We have a myopic view of our work. Should it bear fruit, all hell would break loose. And don't forget about the religious community. How would it play there? We are scientists, though considered crackpots even by many of our peers. In science, if it can be done, it should be done, and then the ethical and moral implications can be addressed in the larger political context, after which it can be dealt with or suppressed."

They spent the rest of the day tinkering with the equipment and on breaks continued to chew over the implications of their discovery.

"Let's call it a day," said Laurenz. "I'm bushed and not a little stymied."

VII

OTHEREARTH ELSEWHERE

22 AMA *

Allfather Bakel made his way through the maze of buildings that characterized old Charlsted City and stopped at an inconspicuous doorway. He knelt and felt the side of the doorframe. His finger found the recessed latch, which he pressed. With the passage of a few seconds, the door opened, and he slipped inside.

He addressed the man who came forward to greet him. "Laurenz, I felt I should check in and brief you on the Congregation's latest neurotic purge of dissidents. Many innocents have gotten caught up in it, and I haven't been able to exercise, even discreetly, a modest influence on the Council."

"I know about that, and it worries me, but I have been distracted by some recent developments," said Laurenz. "You must remember the trans world experiments we have been doing for some time. Quite unexpectedly, and with the initiative of another world, they have been successful. Most specifically, we have made contact with a sister world by coincident or perhaps accidental use of the same experimental technology. Through this, we have transmitted universal

---

*   AMA: *Anno Miraculum Adventus* marked the beginning of The Enlightened Benevolent Dominance of the Theocracy.

symbols, along with hints of a way toward to a more advanced mode of contact. The next step is to attempt a visit. Of course, we can't go there physically, but we have developed a proxy, a functioning hologram, and believe we can indeed go there through the link in that form."

"I see," said Bakel slowly. "At the time, I did not take you seriously. Now that you have shown it possible and actually revealed the existence of another world, it has broad implications with regard to the foundations and doctrine of the Church itself. But does it relate in any way to the aims of the insurgency?"

"Yes," said Laurenz. "If we can make contact and motivate our counterparts in another world to our cause, we may be able to elicit their aid and launch the insurgency from there where the Congregation cannot neutralize it. We can encourage or . . . manipulate, if you will, the creation of functioning surrogates in the form of holograms. Of course, we could make the holograms here, but the principal, the brain of it, must be secluded and free from danger and discovery. As you know, we are constantly on the alert for a raid and have escape routes handy in case of one. Locating the principal one here leaves it and the technology which generates it vulnerable."

"It sounds interesting," said Bakel. "But how will you get strangers to engage our movement. This . . . this other world may be thoroughly stable, in which case the turmoil we experience will be a curious abstraction, or it could have such problems of its own that we wouldn't—not to mention the fact that no one there would—want to take on additional burdens."

"That may be the case. We just have to assess their situation," said Laurenz. "If the issues are perceived as benign, perhaps only a little . . . persuasion may be in order."

Earth

It came suddenly, an intrusion into the recesses of his awareness, an annoying inconvenience jabbing its insolent presence into the tranquility of his slumber. Was it one of those precipitant dreams that happens in a microsecond during REM sleep or something real? Laurenz' reason slowly took over.

The doorbell, he thought. *Nobody rings a doorbell this time of night unless it's some kind of emergency.* Slipping on his robe, he stalked bleary-eyed out to his front door and looked through the peep hole. Somebody—a person—was there. His face was shadowed, because what light there was came from the street behind, and curiously, what he could see of him in the semidarkness was circumscribed with a faint halo. *Should I slip the safety chain from its slot? Leave it,* he said to himself. He opened the door a crack, and light from inside streamed out of the narrow opening illuminating his intruder. He gazed at the person who had disturbed his tranquility. It was him, perhaps a caricature but definitely a replica of him.

How do I respond to seeing myself in the flesh for the first time? thought Laurenz, looking closer at the apparition. *Not exactly flesh, but close enough to scare the wits out of the unexpecting.*

The phantom broke the spell.

"Are you Mr. Laurenz Kapro?" said the thing with a strange, almost mechanical accent.

"I am," said Laurenz, resisting the temptation to say, "at least one of them." He searched frantically for something else to say as full lucidity had finally overtaken his nocturnal stupor.

"My name is also Laurenz. I am your counterpart in a parallel universe or, to be accurate, an electronic likeness thereof projected into your world," said the figure. "In this form, I am an exact analog of my real self. I have the same powers of initiative and am for all practical purposes the Laurenz Kapro of that world. I have come as the first contact to . . . interact for our mutual benefit."

Just like that, thought Laurenz. *Out of the blue comes this being and blithely claims to be from another world. And what was that gibberish about our mutual benefit? With only one significant variation in appearance, it is a perfect rendition of me in the raw—that is, of the raw I can see. Just like the image in the seventh reflection, the man has no hair, a feature in itself not likely to attract attention. That faint halo is practically invisible amid the stronger ambient illumination.*

Laurenz took him at his word. *This thing must be what he just said—a hologram, a functioning replica of an inhabitant of a parallel world with volition of its own. It could pass for real anywhere.*

"How can I help you?" asked Laurenz, in instant chagrin that on such a singular occasion he had resorted to the jargon of a department store clerk.

"I have come from a world existing in tandem with your own both in response to your probe and by way of it," said the alternate Laurenz. "Had you yourself not responded to our effort, we would have remained eternally apart. We have posited that within the infinite array of parallel universes, there is a subset of infinite worlds existing side by side, each with a Laurenz Kapro and other correlates having minute or multiple differences. We are but one of these. You, perhaps, have reached the same conclusions."

"Are you saying that you came to us through the mirror setup at the lab?" said Laurenz.

"Yes," said the alternate Laurenz. "We waited till it was deserted to make the transfer in solitude since we were afraid witnessing the process firsthand would jar the sensibilities of any observer."

"Without a doubt," said Laurenz. "It would have left us all shook up. As to our initial probe, it was by accident, but we were unable to trace effect back to cause. We first received the geometric images in our entanglement chambers, and it was enough to suggest there was an entity there with some degree of intelligence striving for contact."

"That was our first probe," said the alternate Laurenz. "But we had been working on something different, contact through insertions into a gap in multiple reflections. Your contact gave us the . . . the coordinates, for want of a better term, to apply that approach. Initially, having no idea who might respond, we avoided the specifics of language, opting for a more universal form of communication. We tried apparently with success to send directions by way of the images that appeared in your lab. It was our hope that you would find a way forward from the hints in the heptagonal image we sent."

"That worked somewhat," said Laurenz. "One of my team pointed out the similarity between the last image and the reflections created by opposing mirrors, but it can only be considered a chance observation that made us take it seriously. The images from the lab were a refinement of similar images seen by accident in another place of exceptional singularity, a restaurant of all places decorated with large mirrors placed in opposition to one another. I guess it's obvious why you didn't transfer there. Other than that," continued Laurenz, "whatever made you to think you could interact that way? And having decided that course, why not just send a message?"

"You can't escape the mystery inherent in repeating reflections," said the alternative Laurenz. "We found that quite unexpectedly, the quantum disturbances they generate are just as profound as the common sense perception of the phenomenon. Regarding the message, we know only now from firsthand inspection that our worlds were similar enough to share a common language. Since we had the capability to cast ourselves in the form of a hologram, we decided we had nothing to lose by visiting our sister world firsthand."

As he stared at the apparition, Laurenz mulled over what he had just said. *First of all, to keep things straight I'll dub him Alternative Laurenz.* He slowly reached out toward his counterpart. His hand met something solid to the amusement of his guest. *Not flesh, but definitely firm and impenetrable.*

"It is part of our capability," said Alt. Laurenz in answer to the question unasked.

"How do you do that?" said an incredulous Laurenz.

"We first transfer and then impart density to our form by gleaning from the local environment carbon and other elements from plant growth and hydrogen from atmospheric moisture and transform it into a generic polymer," said Alt. Laurenz. "We guessed that it would pass casual inspection and suffice for an occasional bump into an occupant of a target world."

"Okay. Now, just what is your counterpart doing back in your world?" said Laurenz with a tinge of disgust. "Is he acting independently from you or . . . or is he in seclusion sealed in some box while you are here doing your thing?"

"Quite naturally, he is not acting independently," replied a still amused Alt. Laurenz. "He is sequestered in a quiescent chamber insulated from all outside sensory stimulation but controls through me what is going on here. He is to all purposes me, and I he, and for the sake of clarity and simplicity, I shall use first person 'I' as if he were actually speaking."

Laurenz, taking it all in and now shocked to full alertness, was struggling for something to say. He realized to his dismay that he had not considered thoroughly what would happen if they ever actually made contact with a parallel world. It was supposed to be an orderly process, some primitive contact like they had originally received in the entanglement chamber proceeding to exchange of information with the hope of devising a language for communication.

"I have to ask, what do you want here?" said Laurenz.

With ever so slight a pause Alt. Laurenz picked it up. "We—and I use the word *we* to refer to the team of scientists responsible for the contact—we thought in the interest of progress and the pursuit of knowledge in general, you would like to visit our world and perhaps, uh, incorporate any advantages you might find there into your own. And with your permission, we might do the same."

Laurenz laughed. "There are several problems with that," said Laurenz, struck with the naivety of it and a gnawing feeling that Alt. Laurenz was leaving something out. "You are talking about social engineering. I am a scientist. It's not my bag—uh, that is, it's not what I do." *For now, at least, I must stick to Standard English.* "In practice, the only thing that could be done is to record the various aspects of our respective civilizations and bring them back for consideration."

"Yes, I suppose that's true," said Alt. Laurenz. "But in the beginning, somebody has to be the first to show that the transfer can be made at all, and we as scientists are the ones to do that."

"All very well, but on our end, we have a long way to go," said Laurenz. "We would have to fabricate from scratch the technology of making and inserting a functioning hologram into your world, not to mention giving it substance upon arrival."

"I can help you with that," said Alt. Laurenz.

"Okay," said Laurenz after a long pause. "I will first have to introduce you to my colleagues. I hope they don't freak out when they see you. Come to think of it, I better call them first, fill them in, and warn them they are about to see another me. They have already seen the image of your face in the reflection series, and that should soften the impact. So . . . what will you do in the meantime?"

"I will wander around the minute sample of your world available to me," said Alt. Laurenz. "I don't need a place to sleep, but back in my world, my real self does. During that period, I am dormant and immobile, so I only need someplace to remain inconspicuous during this interval."

"Hmm . . . let's not push our luck. All we need is something unforeseen to set off a scary event like some joker mistaking you for dead . . . . No, you had better come to the lab during your period of dormancy. For now, come inside and sit in a nice, comfortable chair." *Not that it would make any difference; he could just stand around,* thought Laurenz. "I must finish my own normal sleep cycle to be fresh tomorrow."

The apparition moved inside with no more exchange and settled in the chair. Laurenz eyed it warily and returned to his bedroom.

VIII

Laurenz awoke and peeked out his bedroom door to assure himself he had not dreamed it all. Alt. Laurenz sat staring off in space but focused on Laurenz when the door opened.

"Give me a minute to get dressed," said Laurenz. "I can grab a bite to eat on the way the lab, but first I have to call Nate, my colleague."

Laurenz grabbed his cell phone. "Nate, you are probably just stirring, but I had to warn you of the latest development. You are not going to believe this, but my otherworld correlate—the ephemeral, whole-bodied version of the one in the seventh reflection—showed up at my door last night. Not his actual physical self, but a reasonable facsimile of it."

There was a choking sound of incoherence on Nate's end.

"You need to quell the multitude of questions you have and just meet me—that is, us—at the lab. Call Sye and fill him in. We need to sit down with . . . me—that is, the other me—and sort this out."

Nate's muddle subsided. He started to say something and then hesitated. "Okay, I'll call Sye. See you there."

Nate quickly dressed and, living closer to the lab, reached there first. His eyes widened as Laurenz and his double entered the lab. He watched as Alt. Laurenz passed in and out of the shadowed areas and didn't miss the ebb and swell of the aura that surrounded him. He groped for some form of address as the alternative Laurenz broke the ice.

"I am happy to meet you. I have explained to Laurenz how I came to be here."

Nate was at a loss to respond and Laurenz picked it up as Sye arrived at the lab.

"My counterpart here, whom I will call Alternative Laurenz . . . maybe . . . Alaurenz is less awkward, if that's all right with you," said Laurenz, turning to his double, who, after a slight hesitation, nodded.

"Also for clarity, it may also be of help if you speak of my world as, say, Otherearth," said Alaurenz. "After all, we have so much in common that we can both claim the appellation Earth."

"A good idea," said Laurenz. "Now, he that is Alaurenz has explained to me the details of his transfer here and is trying to get me to go there using the same technology. As you can see, my friend here is an analog of my alternative's self in his world. I would go in the same form—if, with his help, we can ever get the technology together."

Nate finally found his voice. "You know our budget. If the technology is expensive, how can we do it? What's involved anyway?"

"Two basic things: devising a functioning holographic representation of one of us and the method of insertion into the reflection series," said Laurenz.

"Do we have a leg up on either of those things?" asked Sye.

"No, but we have Alaurenz here to tell us what to do," said Laurenz. "As a practical matter, we will have to do it from the bottom up and glom ideas and hardware from other projects. As to the expense, maybe we can do a budget version of it. I would add that Alaurenz has the ability to impart substance as to his form to disguise some spooky features of his real aspect. If we venture to his world, we may need to do the same. I do not need to remind you that the things he may teach us would be the envy of the government, especially the military, if you get my drift. Therefore, these new developments must be a closely guarded secret."

"Where will the UMC come in?" asked Nate. "You know we have to give them progress reports. Till now we have devised some ephemeral gobbledygook that seems to satisfy them. Do we tell them about this?"

"We may have to," said Laurenz. "But we can couch it in terms of the occult, and they won't know what's really going on. For now, let's concentrate on working with Alaurenz."

"So where do we start?" asked Sye.

Alaurenz broke in. "I can outline and detail what you need to accomplish the things you have mentioned. My form will not permit a hands-on participation. Tactile sensations have not been included in the menu of sensory functions we thought necessary for this mission, though in retrospect it may have been better to have done so. We will consider it when devising your emissary. But to start at the beginning, the process of insertion is accomplished by . . ."

The group was busy in the lab. Several days passed as they stitched together the technology under Alaurenz' tutelage.

"Yes," Laurenz answered as his cell phone rang.

"My name is Christian," the voice on the other end of the line replied. "I would like to speak to Mr. Laurenz Kapro."

"Christian, this is Laurenz speaking. I was wondering when you were going to show up. Marcia didn't even mention that you were here."

"Actually, I have been here for some time—since the beginning of the summer session. I wanted to get acquainted with the school and city before taking the plunge in the fall, so I am taking only a course or two for orientation. I was wondering if I could visit you at the lab."

"Uh—it's a bad time, but . . . let me get back to you."

"Okay, I will look forward to hearing from you."

Laurenz disconnected, "Now, where were we? Oh yes," he said, somewhat distracted.

The day passed as the lab trio continued to transcribe the tech jargon of another world to something familiar. After hours of back and forth, Sye was moved to say, "Well I'll be damned. He's talking about a beam splitter. That's what I called Laurenz about—to somehow harness that aspect of the interferometer."

"Okay, we have an idea of how to insert the thing. How do we make it an analog of a real person?" asked Nate.

"You need to tap the motor, visual, and hearing capacities of the brain of the primary—and, of course, the cognitive functions," said Alaurenz. "The other sensual capacities like smell, feel, and taste are irrelevant and even an impediment. You do this by isolating the primary and drawing from the brain the electrical signals that define these functions. These definitions are then inserted into the holographic representation. I will instruct you in the procedure and instrumentation that will enable you to do this."

"Okay, now tell me this," said Laurenz. "Why do you need to put a likeness of the original in the correlate? Wouldn't any form do?"

"It would, but there is a harmony in the essence of a person," said Alaurenz. "His aspect as a whole is revealed as a composite of his mental and physical characteristics. We have judged it is best to combine the two."

"All right," said Laurenz with a tinge of wariness. "I'll take your word for it. Come to think of it, another identity would require at least some model. We might as well settle on something familiar."

The lab fell into a routine. A place was made for Alaurenz to use in his dormant periods, and those periods were dubbed "recreational." As explained by Alaurenz, his real correlate could not remain inert indefinitely when functioning as a primary for the hologram. He had to break for exercise, nourishment, and interaction with his colleagues on Otherearth. After much back and forth, he was persuaded that to roam around as a Laurenz look-alike could have a disastrous result. The lack of hair made him stand out, which then drew attention to the fact that he was in all other respects an exact likeness of a familiar fixture of the community.

It was now mid-July. Before going any further, there were a couple of things Laurenz had to do.

He sighed as he picked up the phone. "Marcia, can you come over to the lab with me? And perhaps you better bring Christian."

"Sure thing. Christian is in his own orbit. I didn't even know he was here until I accidently met him on campus. Imagine that—my own brother. I'll see if I can get hold of him. In any case, it's about time you told me about the mysterious goings on there. You used to talk about it all the time, and lately you have clammed up. Is there something I need to know?"

"Well, yes. I will do better than that and show you."

"Some new gadget—I can't wait," said Marcia in feigned glee.

"That and more," responded Laurenz cryptically. "When can I pick you up?"

"Noon is okay. My class ends then, and there is a break before my next one."

Laurenz was waiting when Marcia finished class, and they strolled over to the lab.

"Christian will meet us at the lab," said Marcia. "He was very excited about working with you or whatever you have in mind."

"Yes, I think I can work him in. We have a lot of mundane tasks around the lab, and he is just what we need so we can concentrate on the theoretical aspects of the project. At the same time, he can learn on the job. Now, I haven't told you any of this, not because I didn't trust you but because I have been trying to sort it out myself." Laurenz took a breath. "You remember the image you saw in the seventh reflection at Colombo? It was like a bust of me. Well, about six weeks ago the version, 'Laurenz complete,' showed up at my door in the middle of the night—a head to toe replica of myself only with the same bald head and shimmering aura surrounding his being that saw in the reflection."

"Where is it now?" asked a subdued Marcia.

"You are going to meet him at the lab," said Laurenz. "I just didn't want you to be disturbed when you saw him—that is, it."

Marcia, never at a loss for words, indicated by silence that Lawrence had at last found something to disrupt her steady composure. They entered the lab. Alaurenz was sitting alone by the workbench. The island of illumination masked the ever-present aura surrounding him. Nate and Sye had broken for lunch, and the three of them were alone.

"Marcia, I would like you to meet my likeness, Laurenz. For clarity, we call Alaurenz, short for Alternative Laurenz. He is a hologram of my real alternative back in his world."

"It is my pleasure, Miss Amaral. I have heard so much about you."

Without missing a beat, Marcia replied, "It is my pleasure. I hope your jokes are better than Laurenz.'"

"Unfortunately, my fellows back home, if I may oversimplify the citizenry and their location, have little sense of humor, which may in small way relate to the reason I am here," responded Alaurenz.

Now that's a weird thing to say, thought Laurenz as the conundrums surrounding Alaurenz continued to pile up.

Laurenz was relieved to finally bring Marcia in on his mysterious activity. Summer was fading fast, and they had made remarkable strides at the lab. The hologram representing him had been established with the necessary brain functions taken, inserted, and tested in trial runs.

"We will impart substance to your form when you arrive," said Alaurenz. "When I am done here, I will shut down my hologram, and all that will remain is the shell of my organic fill. I will leave it to you to dispose of it."

IX

Laurenz lay sequestered in his chamber. He looked up at the reflection series and saw his hologram repeated continuously to the seventh reflection but not beyond. Suddenly, the view changed. He was aware of being in two places at once but felt he must concentrate on being his "other" self. He knew it was his hologram, as he found himself looking back down toward the observers. Sye and Nate were standing there consumed with uncertainty and looking in his direction.

I feel like I am sandwiched between a pair of . . . something. It must be purely psychological—a delusory claustrophobia induced by the insertion in the reflection series. The process . . . how had Alaurenz described it? "By virtue of the devices we have constructed that bring about a manipulation of reality whose nature we ourselves have yet to fully understand, you will complete the transition and find your hologram situated in the mirror confinement of the alternate world as if it were the original source of the reflection."

In some mysterious way, by virtue of Alaurenz' ultras-science and seemingly in defiance of the principle of cause and effect, he had arrived in another world. Glancing to the side, he saw others were there.

Alaurenz had said "Just step out," thought Laurenz.

Laurenz advanced one holographic limb tentatively and then another with more confidence. Despite his practice runs as a hologram back on Earth, he felt a sensation akin to vertigo. Emerging into the apparent launching point of the experiments from the alternate world, he was greeted by the real-life counterpart of the Alaurenz who had appeared in his world and a delegation of his colleagues.

"We extend greetings and rejoice in the natural kinship between our world and yours, without which a link could not have been established."

Laurenz figured he must respond in kind but already sensed that this world, while superficially like his own, was suffused with an infinite number of differences.

"It is my pleasure, as the first envoy from my world, to receive your warm greeting with hopes that there will be a continuous flow of mutually beneficial information between us," said Laurenz in matching formality.

The ice has been broken, thought Laurenz. *Now to the business of the day, whatever it is.*

Most of the entourage melted into the recesses of the lab, leaving Laurenz alone with Alaurenz the real, but Laurenz noticed a few watching unobtrusively from a distance.

"I will show you around the environs nearby to give you a sense of where you are," said Alaurenz. "But first we must impart substance to your form to make you undetectable."

I guess that's to be expected, thought Laurenz, fears of the unknown welling up in spite of the awareness that his real flesh and blood self was secluded in silence back on his world.

Alaurenz led Laurenz to a chamber and enclosed him within.

"This won't hurt a bit," said Alaurenz, displaying a whiff of humor that had been conspicuously absent in his holographic form.

The process seemed simple, belying the advanced technology that enabled it. He was in and out of the chamber, and when he emerged, there was no subjective feeling of being solid, but as he brushed the edge of the entry to the chamber, he was aware of something pushing back.

"You now have a certain degree of solidity but little dexterity," said Alaurenz. "Your physical acuity is constrained by the limitations of your holographic form. You and your principal back on your world will find that movements exceeding the ordinary will feel like they are being executed under water. This would apply to fast action or the excessively complex movement required for sports, dance, or self-defense. So be aware of your limitations.

"When you think you are ready, I would like to give you a short tour of a brief but important sample of our world."

They left the place that housed the transfer apparatus and wandered outside. Laurenz took in the surroundings. *The Otherearth lab is not contained any kind of educational institution but in a set of buildings resembling an old-fashioned industrial complex on Earth. There are subtle differences. Each facade, cornice, and decorative feature is at the same time familiar and unfamiliar. Apparently the harmony common to Earth and Otherearth has its limits.*

They zigzagged in and out of the maze of buildings.

"Where are we going?" asked Laurenz with the frivolous abandonment of one on an exotic vacation.

"To the Hall of Supreme Knowledge and Authority," responded Alaurenz.

What place could possibly be assigned such a pompous name? But why not? It should be a blast, thought Laurenz.

They moved from the complex where the lab was located into a residential area. Children played, and mothers gossiped while tending to strollers. The scene gave a sense of real Earth normalcy, but the same subtle differences permeated the scene, each element contrasting with the familiar and drawing attention to itself.

Spires of a large edifice peeked over a neat row of tall trees and intervening fauna. Laurenz began to notice a sprinkling of black-clad individuals standing about for no apparent reason. Taken one at a time, their dress in itself was not unusual, because it mimicked that of the average white-collar worker, or what passed for it in his own world. It was the uniformity and omnipresence of the figures which attracted attention. Laurenz was about to inquire about it when they reached a wide, paved pedestrian way of two lanes that led to an opening in the wall of trees. In the distance lay the spired structure in its full magnificence, obviously a temple of some sort. The pedestrian traffic seemed to be going mostly one way—toward the temple.

Laurenz found himself whispering to his companion, "Is that The Hall of . . . of whatever?"

"Yes," replied Alaurenz. "It is the commanding seat of The Devine Congregation of Infinite Wisdom and Compassion, the theocracy that rules us. It is the power behind the national government, deceptively called by the secular name The Confederation of the People. But decrees and enforcement agencies originate with the Congregation and are enforced by the Association of Guardians, a combination of secret police and army. They have shaky symbiotic relationship with the Congregation. In general, here on Otherearth each country is isolated and self-contained. There is little social, commercial, or political interaction between them, a model that perpetuates localized tyranny."

The gigantic size of the temple could now be discerned. The intervening distance was greater than that suggested by the hint of its disassociated spires seen peeking above the trees earlier. It loomed still larger as they approached. If it were possible to merge art deco with the gothic, perhaps the temple could serve as a prototype. The facade, featuring concentric, cane-like arcs that looped and stacked one upon another reaching ever higher, was punctuated by medieval-like elements resembling gargoyles and harpies. The entrance was surmounted by an arch of gothic design, which implied similar elements inside, but the absence of flying buttresses or external shoring meant different principles had been applied for support. Curiously, there seemed to be a consonance in the overall design.

Alaurenz paused near the entrance and spoke in low tones. "I have brought you here to illustrate firsthand the main problem we face here on Otherearth. The pilgrims you see around you are drawn here not by faith or choice but by the not-too-subtle manipulation of the ruling powers."

"You didn't mention this problem before in your altruistic spiel about interaction, but what you speak of is nothing new," said Laurenz with levity. "In our world, there is a constant wax and wane of those who seek power through legitimate or devious means and coax those vulnerable to their view by subtle propaganda."

"No doubt, but here it is evil, universal, and unless arrested, permanent," said Alaurenz with a seriousness that jarred Laurenz' lighthearted exuberance and suddenly diminished his joy at just being there through a novel scientific breakthrough.

"Danvar is the seat of that power and capital of the Consolidated States of America. It is from here that The Divine Congregation rules both locally and through tendrils extending to the provinces."

Laurenz was beginning to feel he was getting himself into something that went beyond a simple tour of a parallel world.

"Well, how does it affect you? You seem to be free to do as you wish."

Alaurenz' eyes panned to the left and right of Laurenz and then concentrated on him.

"We in our group are free of the influence and corruption that infects all society. I will explain it to you in due course, but first I must give you a sample of what we are up against. You may have noticed the cadre of uniformed men standing about."

"Yes, as a matter of fact I did," said Laurenz.

"They are the Guardians of Righteousness, the secret police of the theocracy. We must steer clear of them at all costs."

In the innards of the temple, Allfather Flecthrum, with the help of two acolyte assistants, donned his robes in a cubicle just off the vast enclosure of the cathedral nave. "Is the Becalming Ambience activated?"

"As usual, Your Benevolence."

"And the Cleansing Chamber—is it charged? We don't want another incident like last week when the process was incomplete with the flock so shocked that it nullified the becalming signal."

"It has been checked and checked again," said the acolyte.

X

Cralle sat quietly in the rear of the temple, carefully watching the other pilgrims. He had learned to imitate the conduct of the subdued, but as of now, he had no plan except to survive, and that meant yielding to the periodic summons of segments of the populace to the cathedral. The results of deviant behavior were quite clear, so he strove first of all to blend in with the controlled masses, carefully scheduling and choreographing his periodic visits to the temple.

The thought kept returning: *There must be others out there like me who have not come under the spell of the restraining implant.*

For reasons he had never understood, when he came of age and the time-activated controls in the chip were to take effect, nothing happened. The Congregation made a ritual of the event, a coming-of-age ceremony universally inflicted and promoted at age fifteen. It was the pivotal moment in the movement to manhood. For girls it was imposed earlier, at the average age of menses when childbearing capacity was achieved. This discouraged promiscuity and supported population control.

The service concluded with the daily Cleansing and the Admonishment, after which the faithful filed out of the temple. Cralle observed that control was not relinquished until they had cleared a definite perimeter around the temple and even then only gradually, so he carefully observed the boundaries of this imaginary line. Someone brushed past him, not in haste but definitely out of the regimented pace of the flock. It was a girl.

She had better slow down, he thought.

She moved slowly past several to the front of Cralle and onto the walkway leading away from the temple, but only now were they passing the line of imposed restraint. The anomaly had not been missed by the Guardians. Out of the corner of his eye, Cralle saw a dark figure move from the side into the flow of pilgrims. The gap between pursuer and the pursued was narrowing, and Cralle was forced to make a decision. In his quest to find someone, anyone, who was free of the control, this was the first indication. He picked up his pace. The Guardian reached the girl, planted a hand on her shoulder, and swung her around. In turning she instantly presented an anomalous face of panic to her pursuer. The stream of pilgrims ebbed and flowed around the arrested couple with only a slight indication of delay or concern being still in the never land of partial control. Of those who were partially aware, they had seen it happen before, but instinct always trumped curiosity. The crowd shunned involvement in matters related to the Congregation.

His captive in tow, the Guardian turned. Advancing against the flow, he moved in the direction of the temple.

Cralle made a quick decision. He reached into his pocket and palmed a chrome-colored object. The tethered couple approached slowly against the current of pilgrims that enveloped Cralle. At the moment of passage, he pushed the instrument up under the over jacket of the Guardian. The Guardian crumpled to the walkway and was masked by the human stream. Without missing a beat, Cralle grabbed the girl and spun her around while urging her forward and away from the scene.

"Who—" She choked out only a word before Cralle cut her off.

"Keep going," he force whispered. "The Guardians won't stay unaware long."

A moment later several black-clad agents could be seen converging on the spot they had left behind.

"Let's pick it up a bit, before they detain the whole lot of us," said Cralle, mindful of the indiscriminate sweeps made by the Guardians.

They passed through the wall of trees and swung right on the first artery leading from the main temple walkway. The girl had said nothing, but her physical rigidity and zombie-like gait revealed the extent of her terror. They passed into a residential section where the houses were more closely packed, and the segment of inhabitants who though no more numerous were not at the moment under the spell of the temple imperative or scheduled for it. Cralle chose one of the several coffee shops that peppered the neighborhood in quest of the anonymity such a place might provide.

"Stay here," he ordered the still traumatized girl, gently pushing her into a chair.

He moved to the dispensing counter, never taking his eyes off the girl, ordered two coffees, and returned to the table. He spoke in a low voice. "Now, am I wrong, or are you free of the restraints of the Congregation?"

The girl hesitated, but having recovered some composure, she spoke. "Who are you? Maybe you are also of the Guardians and in some sinister plot to uncover a deviant cell by entrapping a member."

"Cralle, Cralle Damon," he said, ignoring her suspicions. "I think I have guessed right. Your reactions to the Guardian gave you away. You blew it by your errant actions when leaving the Church. You know that is a hot spot where they carefully judge behavior during the wane of the suppression signal."

The girl was quiet for a time, studying Cralle's face for some clue as to his sudden appearance and motives. Cralle sat patiently and waited for some response.

"My name is Janize Glanzer. If . . . I were in conspiracy against the Congregation, the Guardians would have been justified in retaining me," she said, still cautious.

"Look, stop playing games. You were almost taken in. They have ways of exposing us," said Cralle with a lump in his throat, realizing he had just exposed himself.

There was a visible sign of relief in the girl. "When did you first realize you were free of the restraints?"

"At fifteen, the age of indoctrination," said Cralle.

"How did you escape detection?" she asked.

"By mimicking those who were."

"But what motivated you to do that? They brainwash us from an early age to accept it as a universal good."

"You know that is never absolute," said Cralle sarcastically. "The young are always questioning everything, and the Congregation has its arms full containing adolescent behavior. If it weren't for the disastrous results of implanting the chip at birth, we would all be under its grip. And even now after the chip is implanted, the low-level suppression they broadcast continuously to achieve domestic tranquility is subject to blank spots. That explains all the crime and otherwise deviant activity, and it's the reason they ratchet it up from time to time to calm things down. You yourself—how have you escaped detection?"

"I arrived at the institute at the proper time but became ill during the implantation for reasons unrelated to the procedure. I was admitted to a care facility. The records were recorded incorrectly, and I was released unaltered."

"Well—Janize, I have been searching for another like me."

Free now of the anxiety of the moment, he looked at her as if for the first time. His suppressed first impression surfaced. She was somewhat younger than he, small and delicate with a perky, turned-up nose blending harmoniously with a coif of neat blonde hair, which was pulled back and tied with a ribbon. The teal-colored wrap dress she wore drawn tightly at the waist and extending to just below the knee revealed a lithe but shapely figure.

"You must know that to be free of the Congregation's spell, imposed dogma, and behavioral boundaries is a prescription for loneliness. Do you have any friends? Anyone you can really talk to, confide in, or even trust?" Cralle asked. "The organized underground of people like us are constantly under siege. Just look at today's Cleansing. That was a public execution, plain and simple."

"You are right about the loneliness part, and no, I have only transient and superficial friends," said Janize after a pause. "You never know whom you can trust. What did you do to that Guardian back there? Thanks for whatever it was."

"I gave him a dose of the Congregation's technology, which they try to keep under wraps. I was educated in electronics and was able to deduce the basic principles of many of the weapons they use to control the populace and duplicate them for my own use.

"We must form our own little cell if you have the stomach for it," continued Cralle. "There must be an army of others like us who are afraid to surface. Where do you live?"

"On the other side of town in Braddock, near the canal."

"I will see you there, as I do not live far away," said Cralle as they rose to leave. "We must stay in contact. Here is my address and telecom number on this card. But use it only in emergency and even then in coded language and generalities. We are constantly monitored. We can discuss it along the way,"

Laurenz and Alaurenz had joined the flow and entered the temple. The nave soared to breathtaking heights and from a short way up showed honeycombed flanks extended ever higher and over the top, suggesting a geodesic principle of self-contained rigidity and perhaps explained how the enormous structure supported itself. They found the interior already crowded with the faithful sitting in a stupefied solemnity so extreme that it seemed abnormal, even in the cathedral setting, and cast an ominous veil over the proceedings.

What sort of hold does the . . . setting or situation, for want of a better word, have on the multitude, mused Laurenz. In the distance at the center of focus were an enormous altar of sorts and a lone robed figure standing quietly before a podium. He raised his arms and intoned: "Nunc demum redit animus. Corpora nostra cito extinguuntur."

"That is Allfather Flecthrum. He usually presides over the services and uh . . . other events," whispered Alaurenz.

The priest droned on in an impenetrable language. *Sounds like some variation of Latin*, thought Laurenz as he inquired of Alaurenz, "What is he saying?"

"The usual, a subtle warning of the fragility of life then calling to attention the legions of the faithful to obey and respect the authority of the Congregation, which, of course, stems from divine appointment—all this in the traditional language of Sanslatin. At the close, he will deliver a sermon for the day in the vernacular, the English we speak but more formal."

Laurenz looked around at the congregation, which was still in a permanent daze. "What makes the crowd so passive?"

"It is electronically induced through a surgically implanted chip. Those in my group are not affected because of countermeasures, and you, of course, because of your holographic form. In all others, it is activated as they approach and enter and at the will and discretion of the authority at any other time and place they deem necessary for control. Through it, they summon all to the temple, which is not only a place of worship but the center from which all decrees and propaganda in support of the Congregation are dispensed. They supplement this coercion with control of the public media. All news, drama, or features are dumbed down to reinforce the message of compliance."

The service droned on with the speaker lapsing into a form of English to deliver the day's sermon, after which there was an introit ending in a bizarre ritual.

A group of worshipers, no more than four or five, were brought from the innards of the temple and ushered into a cubicle Laurenz had not noticed before, an enclosure with decorative features blending in with the rest of the temple's interior. With the doors now open, its stark interior contrasted with the ornate surroundings. At some signal, there was a sudden restlessness in the sullen crowd.

Alaurenz whispered to Laurenz. "For this demonstration, the control of the chip is attenuated for enhanced effect. Watch."

With the portals to chamber closed, the chant reached its climax, merging with a sharp grating sound that filled the temple. At the signal of the priest, the doors slowly opened for all to see.

Nothing looks much different, thought Laurenz. *There they are as before, just standing there still . . . too still.* But as the seconds wore on, there was a silence in the crowd, which Laurenz knew this time was not artificially induced.

"What has happened?" whispered Laurenz.

"It is essentially a public execution, although they call it a Cleansing Reduction," said Alaurenz. "The victims are suspect or have been caught doing something subversive or downright threatening to the Congregation. They are instantly solidified by transforming the carbon in the body from its essential life-giving function to an inert generic polymer not unlike the process that has given solidity to your hologram. In this case, because it has been applied to a physical form, it means instant death to the subject. Other than a slight change in color, they appear to be still alive. They stage these events as punishment and a warning to the populace."

Laurenz felt a chill, though he knew it was only psychological as his sensory self was not at the temple but back on his home world in seclusion. *What have I gotten myself into?*

Alaurenz broke Laurenz' reverie. "We are finished here. When the service concludes, we will exit with the others but not before. The Guardians are on the lookout for deviants—that is, rebels to the authority of the Congregation. These can take the form of scientists like us or an occasional anomaly, who by some process not understood, has not come under the domination if the nascent implant. Any aberrant behavior can lead to retention, interrogation, and, if lucky, only imprisonment. Otherwise, the result is that which you have just witnessed."

They moved slowly with the masses as they exited the temple, dense now that they were close, but the crowd thinned out as some took to the branching side paths. A figure passing on the right stood out, moving somewhat faster than the steady flow. It all happened fast. The figure, a girl, reached a spot some twenty paces ahead was intercepted by black-clad Guardian who had entered from the side, causing a break in the smooth stream, a transient turbulence that came and went. But when they reached the spot, a Guardian could be seen lying on the pathway with pilgrims moving past, heads turned away.

Alaurenz whispered to Laurenz. "Veer left slightly and keep going. I don't know what happened, but it's best not to get involved."

The girl could still be seen, but she was now accompanied by another who seemed to hustle her along.

"I was going to return to the lab but would if you will indulge me a bit," said Alaurenz. "I wish to follow those two. If my suspicions are correct, they are deviants. Let's lie back a little and see what they do."

The couple moved out of the environs of the temple and into the adjoining neighborhood. They watched them as they entered a modest coffee shop. Laurenz stood uncertainly. *It's like being a virtual participant in a TV drama.* "Well how about some coffee," he said jovially, caught up in the excitement of it and secure that in his present form, he could not be in a dangerous situation.

"All right," said Alaurenz cautiously. "We must be sure that they were not followed by others. The Guardians are not always visible."

They entered, and Laurenz said, "Given the unknowns when I interact with material objects, you better negotiate the coffee while I sit over here and watch the couple . . . and bring me half a cup. I can pretend to drink it."

Laurenz watched the two, now clearly revealed as two adults—a man and a woman who was somewhat younger. They were engaged in intense dialog as Alaurenz arrived at the table. Taking turns eying the couple, a puzzled Alaurenz suddenly stiffened.

"I know what it is," whispered Alaurenz. "The man sitting to their right in the shadows seems to be watching them too, and he doesn't fit in. This place is mostly frequented by college age kids. That guy is older and has 'institutional' written all over him. He could have already been here as a routine stop or entered unnoticed after we came in. The Guardians may have put in an area-wide net for the culprits in the incident on the temple walkway."

They watched as the couple rose and started to leave, followed in quick succession by their watcher. As they approached the exit, the man from the shadows surged forward and blocked their way. The young man fumbled for something in the pockets of his jacket but was restrained by the brute strength of their aggressor. Alaurenz was transfixed by the encounter and frozen to immobility, while Laurenz, responding to some animal urge, converged on the scene. From the rear, Laurenz enveloped the assailant's neck with his right arm. The springy firmness of his polymeric fill held momentarily, but the slowness of his reactions limited his tactical initiative. His advantage was that he could not be hurt. His bulk, which had affixed itself to the Guardian like a doe-filled sack, entangled his adversary, forcing him to release his captive as he flailed frantically as if encapsulated in some super viscous pool. The patrons caught off guard belatedly focused in on the scene and moved in a body to absent themselves in fear they might become involved in one of the Congregation's sweeps.

Janize hesitated a moment too long. By the time she reached the door to the shop, it was clogged with those fleeing. Cralle, now free, joined her and the others funneling to the outside.

"Go! I'll be okay." Laurenz snapped at Alaurenz, at the same time gesturing with his free hand at the struggling couple just now squeezing through the choked exit.

Alaurenz winced but nodded and rushed after the besieged couple.

Laurenz was now practically alone with the Guardian except for a few employees who remained at their stations, frozen witnesses to the scene. The mini-drama in the coffee shop had no obvious conclusion. The Guardian's struggles had managed to transfer Laurenz' weight so that the center of gravity of the intertwined pair was now shifting toward instability. Laurenz fought frantically to maintain equilibrium. Failure came in a crash as the pair toppled over onto a table still strewn with cups, saucers, and plates. The Guardian was quick to recover and was on his feet before Laurenz, in his sloth-like mode, righted himself. The Guardian reached into his inner pocket and pulled out a handheld device, pointed, and activated it against the now erect Laurenz. A flash of light was reflected from Laurenz' body as he turned to go. The Guardian, momentarily puzzled that his first line of offense had not neutralized his adversary, retrieved from the recesses of his jacket a pistol-like weapon and fired at Laurenz' retreating form. A localized portion of Laurenz' upper torso disappeared, revealing an island of his hologram but leaving intact the remainder his polymeric form. The Guardian stood back astonished.

"Who . . . what are you?" he snarled at Laurenz.

Laurenz ignored him as he hurried out the door but was suddenly aware of the downside of his reckless attempt at rescue. Holographic versions of the opposition, or even the technology itself, were apparently unknown to the Congregation, and in spite of all good intentions, he had revealed an important secret. Before the Guardian could decide on additional action, Laurenz had exited and was gone.

Alaurenz left soon after the besieged couple and searched frantically for them amid the random passersby and former patrons fleeing the coffee shop. *There.* He spied the pair rounding the corner of a building some fifty yards to his left. Leaving Laurenz to his own resources, he made after them. Reaching the corner, the couple could be seen scurrying away in the distance. He breathlessly closed the gap and gasped a husky, "Please stop!"

Cralle slowed and turned nervously, fingering his stunner.

"You . . . it was you who intervened in the coffee shop?"

"Not exactly. I will explain later. For now, I will say that I am of the same sort as you," said Alaurenz, still recovering from his frantic pursuit. "It was my . . . my colleague who engaged the Guardian. Follow me to a place of safety, and we can discuss your situation and your options for the future."

Cralle hesitated and looked at Janize who showed uncertainty, then spoke. "Your colleague, it was your twin or—"

"All right, my twin, only you will remember he had hair. That will do for now. His name is Laurenz, as is mine, so get in the habit of calling me Alaurenz to eliminate confusion."

"Okay, but I have weapons of my own to prevent any trickery."

"Follow me," said Alaurenz without comment.

They made their way back through the maze of buildings to the secret hiding place of the lab.

"Your . . . your brother, back there, why did he intervene, and what about his own safety?" asked Cralle.

"He will be all right," said Alaurenz uncertainly. His mind raced with disturbing thoughts. *In spite of Laurenz' immunity to injury, it is to be assumed the Congregation will suspect advanced capabilities in the opposition. If Laurenz had to deactivate his holographic form and just disappear, the shell of his polymeric form will remain for the scrutiny of Congregation's scientists. They would soon deduce that rogue science had produced a functioning surrogate for a real person, resistant to persuasion, weapons, punishment, or death.*

Laurenz looked around but was not surprised that Alaurenz had vanished in pursuit of the couple. *Now where could they have gone?* he wondered. In the excitement of entering a parallel world, he had not noted the labyrinthine route they had taken out from the secluded lab. He regarded the mix of buildings in the direction from which they had come. They appeared more or less of recent vintage, but the random arrangement of narrow, twisting streets suggested that the planners had conformed to the original outline of the city when adding new structures, and the result was a sort of Venice without canals.

Damn, I'm getting tired, thought Laurenz. *Surely he will come looking for me. On the other hand, maybe not, figuring I would likely be followed by the Guardian and others he may have summoned. My wake-sleep cycle is the same as it has always been. If I can't figure out where Alaurenz has gone, I might have to park my sloven holographic self some place in order to rest.*

He waded into the hodgepodge of buildings looking for something familiar—nothing. He spied a large dumpster and eyed it warily. *I could just discard my fill there, deactivate the hologram, and then wait till Alaurenz contacts me and take it from there. Maybe the fill won't be noticed at the disposal facility. It will just look more or less like a department store dummy—with a hole in it.*

As Laurenz could think of nothing better, he looked around and saw only a few people moving away and some crisscrossing the intersections. Slipping the metal cover of the dumpster, he eased himself in and nestled into the refuse.

XI

Laurenz rose from the recliner and extracted himself from the chamber to be met by a quartet of anxious onlookers.

In addition to Sye and Nate, Marcia and Christian were there. Laurenz felt it necessary to assure them that he was perfectly okay.

"So . . . how was it?" asked Nate. The others all had the same question on their faces.

"Did you actually experience another world?" asked Christian.

"I did—and more, which I will tell you about," said Laurenz annoyed and still preoccupied by the damage he may have done. "Unfortunately, it was not the benign travelogue any of us would have expected. To put it briefly, they have problems over there. But for now, it's late and I am bushed, not from physical exertion but from tension related to the transfer. I have to sort it out myself and will fill you in tomorrow morning at say . . . nine thirty. Meet me here and let me know if Alaurenz shows up again. We got separated in the chain of events."

The group nodded a grumpy assent and dispersed.

Laurenz went over to Marcia. "I'm sorry, sweetheart. Let me get some rest, and we can get together in the morning. How about we have breakfast together?"

"That's okay with me," said Marcia. "Maybe we can meet someplace besides the campus cafeteria."

"Right, meet me at Francois. We can have an early brunch and come over to meet the others over here."

Laurenz spent a restless night. Ominous figures bedecked in black business suits continually intruded into his slumber. He rose early in a more resolute state of mind and scurried over to Francois to meet Marcia, who was already there when he arrived. Pensive as they partook of the discreet but tasty offerings of this favorite of off-campus cafes, Laurenz gradually relaxed.

"We must all get together and decide what to do. This thing has the potential of getting out of hand. I was hoping Alaurenz would show up again so we could all have some input."

"I am breathless to hear what happened," said Marcia.

"If you want a preview, we can start with the fight I got into in the coffee shop."

"Fight? How could you possibly fight in the state you entered the other world? If I am to believe you, you had no . . . no substance, or only the kind Alaurenz had after he got here," said Marcia.

"It was enough for me to physically engage one of the villains of the other world. I wasn't very effective, because my movements were reduced to sloth-like, but remember that a hologram cannot be hurt."

"Now that you know how to transfer, can't you just look for another parallel world that doesn't spell trouble?" Marcia asked with a sigh.

The same question dominated the discussion as the group stood around the workbench at the lab.

"We may be able to do that; then again, we may not," said Laurenz. "According to Alaurenz, our contact is based on the close kinship between our worlds in the space-time domain. If there are an infinite number of them, those of similar timeline assume a sort of tangential relationship like two spheres or solid blobs touching at one point, and that point becomes the gate and path of transfer. Perhaps we can regard all other parallel worlds as floating out there and having no common point with us. Of course, the idea 'out there' is only a metaphor. They may exist concurrent and concentric with us—that is, in the same spot, inhabiting dimensions existing in exclusivity."

"What on earth does that mean?" asked Marcia to the chuckles of Sye and Nate.

"Simply that the three dimensions we know may be only an illusion. Look at the zany ideas in string theory with dimensions tiny and curled up so as not to be noticed. In this case, it would be like closed solids, spheres or ellipsoids, touching, each in its makeup having no effect on the other but existing in the same space,"

"That would require a new definition of space," said Nate.

"I'm dizzy," said Christian, who until then had remained silent.

"Back to matters at hand," said Laurenz. "For now, we are committed to Otherearth, even though it is a little galling that Alaurenz did a bait and switch on me," continued Laurenz. "The bait was the lure of a parallel world and the triumph of our efforts, but the switch is a world in great part like ours but with a dark side. What they are dealing with is an oppressive theocracy they call The Congregation of Infinite Wisdom and Compassion, which places them and those not of like mind in mortal danger. Think of Hitler running the Vatican.

"Soon after I transferred, they gave me a polymeric fill, similar to that Alaurenz had when he came here. In the course of my . . . visit, if you can call it that, I became involved in a certain incident that resulted in damage to that form, so I ditched it and deactivated my hologram. I expect—that is, I hope—that Alaurenz will contact me again. He may be miffed because I acted out of impulse and may have compromised their security. I can see what he was getting at, however. When we transfer in holographic form, we are immune to physical threat—to put it simply, we are safe. He views us as potential allies against the Congregation."

"But why didn't he just transfer some of his own people to the holographic form and use them?" asked Nate.

"They probably think that the primary is safer if sequestered on a parallel world," said Laurenz hesitantly. "And they would be hard-pressed to devise a plausible scenario for using one of their own with our help without revealing all, which speaks to the bait and switch issue."

Marcia, who had been silent during the exchange, spoke softly. "But . . . if we can go there as virtual people, why can't they come here in the same form and make mischief?"

"Well, frankly, I had not considered such a possibility. As far as I know, the Congregation doesn't have the technology that Alaurenz and his followers have," said Laurenz, his ruminations stimulating yet another thought: *All it would take is a raid on their facility to get that. If my actions have spawned suspicions, then there will be a witch-hunt and a sweep.* "Besides, what could they do without allies here to mount an insurgency?"

"They could co-opt them, assemble them together like a pickup band," said Marcia. "You know, even here there are always groups: misfits, religious zealots, and anarchists who would welcome any assistance to further chaos even if this world is not open to the kind of universal tyranny you describe. In Brazil they spring up all the time. Many form political parties to achieve legitimacy as a cover."

As they all stood listening, it dawned on them, as it had Laurenz that moving to a parallel world was not only about science. There was silence around the workbench.

XII

The supreme Council of The Devine Congregation of Infinite Wisdom and Compassion met in the Chamber of the Blessed Allfathers, the Archfather Verkezian presiding.

"Blessed and disciples of limitless devotion, it has been reported to me by the Chief of Guardians that an enemy of unknown potential has infiltrated the flock and may pose a threat to us, the purity of our creed, and the stable society that enables us to continue to teach the Path of True Righteousness."

"What is it specifically?" asked Allfather Corvus impatiently. "As Overseer of the Guardians, I must know if it is a real danger. If so, we must cut through this stifling ritual, which weighs on our deliberations like a millstone."

Jarred from the banal formality customary in the sessions, Verkezian responded soberly, "The Guardians report a set of encounters with persons who exhibit immunity to our broadcasts of blanket serenity. One of these was of a singular nature. It seemed to not be of the flesh at all, but some kind of functioning representation of a person. The Diocese of Divine Science informs me that the technology to produce such an entity is known, but before now, no need has emerged to develop it. The Guardians, however, are advising us to petition them to produce something of similar capability."

"Why did I not hear of this?" Allfather Corvus snapped. "Any matter concerning Guardian operations should be reported to me for action."

"The agent involved thought it was a matter for the DDS and went there first," soothed Verkezian. "I am sure you would have been informed—eventually."

"Event-t-t," sputtered an outraged Corvus.

Allfather Leeche broke in. "We know there are those among the flock who are not under our control, but they are scattered and unorganized and have never posed a threat. This . . . this thing the Guardian described, is it really a danger to us? And 'functioning'? How is it functioning? What can it do?"

"That is uncertain," said Verkezian. "Certainly, if it cannot be harmed, we have no control over it. The most it could do is spread counterpropaganda to poison the minds of the flock as they tread the Path of True Righteousness, which is enough. For additional details, we will have to await the formal report from the Guardians and get input from the DDS. Then we can meet again and decide on further action."

Allfather Bakel sat unobtrusively in the rear, taking it all in, nodding, and murmuring assents in the proper places. *What the hell happened? This doesn't sound like anything Laurenz would do. It is too bold. Something got out of hand. I must warn them at once.*

Having escaped the chaos of the café, Alaurenz and the couple wove their way through the maze of buildings and arrived at the discreet doorway, the entrance to the clandestine lab and hiding place of the dissident scientists.

Once inside, Alaurenz introduced them to the staff. "These are our colleagues. All of them have families and legitimate jobs for cover, which they can return to as necessity demands, and are, of course, free of the suppression signal. All are sworn to secrecy. We hope you will join us and think you will, based on my assessment of your recent behavior. I must tell you now that for our protection, there are consequences for not doing so."

"And what are they?" asked Cralle

"Nothing fatal," said Alaurenz. "Just memory erasure, but there are unpredictable side effects from that."

"You needn't worry," said Cralle. "I have been looking for people like you. I am surprised you have remained undetected."

"It hasn't been easy, but it is helped by using the Congregation's own technology against them. We ourselves broadcast a low-level suppressant during incursions into this area, configured so that it dulls the Guardian's cognitive functions. So far, it has worked. It is so subtle they don't even know they are being manipulated."

A quiet chime sounded, and Laurenz went to the portal that gave entrance to the lab. The robed figure of Allfather Bakel entered. Cralle reflexively reached for his stunner as he recognized the garb and accouterments of the Congregation priest.

"It's okay," said Alaurenz. "Bakel, you could not have come at a more opportune time." He turned to address Cralle and Janize. "I would like for you to meet Allfather Bakel, our ally, a mole sympathizer within the Congregation's ranks. He warns us of impending sweeps."

Allfather Bakel approached the group and spoke hastily as he fidgeted with the inverted cross** that hung matinee length from his neck. "Some incident has set off the Guardians and alerted the Council of a threat to the Congregation. What has happened?"

"The trans world experiments mentioned during our last meeting have progressed to the next stage," said Alaurenz. "I have made contact with my counterpart in this other world by visiting it in a holographic form. We have informed them of these methods, and they are now able to visit here in the same cast. As to what happened, I can tell you only to a certain point, as it involved the attempted arrest of my two

** The martyred savior symbolized by the cross was crucified upside down.

young friends here, in which my counterpart from the other earth intervened. In my pursuit of the two, I was separated from him, so the details and resolution of the encounter are unknown at this time. My guess is that he discarded the shell that gave him substance and deactivated his hologram. He is probably waiting for me to make contact again."

"Let me know when that happens," said Bakel. "We may be able to plant him somewhere in the bureaucracy of the Congregation where my status as Defender of the Faith forbids me to go—that is, if we can motivate him to do so. Archfather Verkezian has cleverly partitioned the clergy responsibilities to prevent the free flow of information and sharing of doctrinal differences. If your counterpart shares your scientific expertise, I can try to maneuver him into the Diocese of Divine Science. If we can get in there, it may be possible, at least locally, to sabotage the suppression broadcasts for good and preempt any other advance in control technology. If this is successful, we will have a restricted time window to organize the latent resentment of the public to the tyranny of the Congregation and coax those in the outlying provinces still under control to follow our example. Now, does your counterpart closely resemble you?"

"Quite closely, only he has a full head of hair," said Alaurenz.

"Hmm . . . look-alikes occur all the time," said Bakel. "In the event of a sweep, that plus proof that you were in another place at the time of an 'incident' would probably keep you safe from retention by the Guardians, but to be safe, you should avoid public exposure. I must return to the Cloister. If and when you make contact, notify me. I will meet with him. We must plan. I have no active allies within the ranks of the clergy. They are either basking in the power of the Congregation or afraid to go up against the establishment. Some, however, secretly share my views of the faith run amuck. I must go now. Keep me informed."

Archfather Verkezian sat in conference with the Leader of the Diocese of Devine Science, Adjunctfather Jurse Romarda, and Chief of Guardians Lauf Ganderk. He addressed the scientist.

"What can you tell us about the peculiar form our agent encountered in the coffee shop?" asked Verkezian.

"From what Chief Ganderk tells me, I have concluded that rogue scientists have produced a functional hologram and given it substance to enable it to blend in with the populace," said Romarda.

"The agent blew away a portion of the artificial filling imparted to it," said Ganderk. "It revealed the bare image, but due to its nature, the thing was left fully functional, as the controlling essential was hidden elsewhere. To neutralize it, we must find the essential source."

"Can we do this?" said Verkezian.

"We can develop instrumentation to detect the controlling stream of the hologram and perhaps track it to its origin," said Romarda.

"That would certainly shorten the process," said Ganderk. "Otherwise, we will have to sweep every cranny in each neighborhood, which would take months, although my guess is that they are operating from the maze of buildings in Old Town."

"Let's see if we can track it without doing a sweep and stirring up the populace," said Verkezian. Turning to Romarda, he added, "When can you have the equipment ready?"

"A week, maybe sooner."

XIII

Alaurenz arrived at the Earth lab, stepped out of the mirror arrangement, and gleaned from the environment the necessary ingredients to make his holographic form solid. Light filtering through a window cast dim shadows that crisscrossed the floor of the forest of connections essential to the machinery of transfer. He glanced at his watch and went dormant.

The next day Laurenz was the first to arrive at the lab. As he neared, he spied Freda Freeland approaching from the opposite direction. Her long black hair hung loose and had split; half draped over the right side, partially concealing a stark ghostly face with no makeup except on her lips, while the other half disappeared behind her left shoulder. With each step, the swish of her ankle-length floral dress combined rhythmically with the jingle jangle of her multiple beads.

Christ, what a bad time. I'll just have to endure it. I'll feed her just enough to give the impression that we are in contact with the mysterious infinite.

"Freda! What a pleasure to see you. I've been anxious to bring you up to date on what we have been doing. Come inside the lab."

In his preoccupied state, he almost missed the motionless figure of Alaurenz standing unobtrusively to the side. Momentarily startled and forgetting Freda, he snapped, "Don't do that! Make some . . . some noise or something. You scared the crap out of me."

"The what?" Alaurenz questioned.

"Never mind," said Laurenz, again realizing that the linguistic symmetry between the two worlds had its limits. *Again, crap. How can I explain him to Freda? He looks just like me.*

"Freda, this is my bother—you can probably see the family resemblance," said Laurenz limply.

"Why yes, I do indeed see a resemblance."

Alaurenz, sensing he may have appeared at an inappropriate time, settled for a benign, "It is a pleasure to meet you. Good morning, Laurenz."

"Uh . . . Al, would you give me a minute? I have to show Ms. Freeland around," said Laurenz, not wanting to confuse the situation.

"Certainly," said Alaurenz with his familiar mischievous smirk. He turned away and pretended to busy himself in a remote corner of the lab.

"Your brother, is he involved in the project too?" asked Freda.

"Uh, as a matter of fact yes," said Laurenz, anxious to change the subject. "Now, I am happy to inform you that we have signs of a breakthrough. Some mysterious signs have appeared in our chambers, and we are endeavoring to respond. We are sure they are signals from another world or . . . from the departed."

"Oh my goodness, at long last," said Freda. "We of the coalition always knew we would eventually commune with the Infinite."

"Well, we are not sure exactly what it is," said Laurenz, pulling back with the thought, *Just where are we going with this?*

"As representative of my followers, I would be privileged to be in attendance in the consummate moment of contact. Could it be arranged?"

"Why, uh yes . . . y-y-yes, of course," stammered Laurenz. "I will notify you when the sacred moment is at hand."

"I will inform the coalition of your progress," said Freda, who then left on a cloud.

"I guess you heard that," said Laurenz as he approached Alaurenz. "I haven't mentioned it before, but we are considered a little off the mainstream in regard to scientific research and have resorted to . . . unconventional sources for financial support."

"I understand perfectly," said Alaurenz with a face strained but contained, because the capacity for tears was not programed into his holo form.

Laurenz glared at the off-worlder, looking for a reason to blast him but decided to change the subject.

"In any case, we have been waiting and are glad you are back. I must apologize for the incident at the coffee shop. I acted on impulse and only now can imagine the repercussions of it."

"It is worse than you think," said Alaurenz, suddenly serious. "It has alerted the Congregation to our ability to field holographic surrogates of the insurgency and will give them a target more clearly defined—the scientific community. Our contact within the clergy has verified this."

"I am truly sorry. Is there anything I can do?" asked Laurenz, regretting it immediately.

"Well, yes," said Alaurenz. "You—"

The door opened, revealing Nate and Sye who had arrived together. They stared at their visitor with the same expressions of awe as before.

"Alaurenz was just bringing me up to date on what has happened since I left Otherearth," said Laurenz.

"You can continue to let us operate from here," said Alaurenz. "We are vulnerable as long as we mount opposition from Otherearth. Here, you are insulated from reprisal by the dimensional barrier between us. If they find our base of operations in Old City where we sequester primaries, we will be greatly compromised, but we can retire to our prime facility on the outskirts of the city and operate from there. We can duplicate the mirror arrangement for interworld transfer, but even then there is the potential for discovery. If we can continue to operate from off world, all they can discover is a pile of equipment. If you and your companions care to participate in our cause, we would be most appreciative; otherwise, we are restrained from using this new tool to break the grip of the Congregation."

"You are talking about fighting some kind of guerrilla war," said an irritated Laurenz. "I am a little miffed that you sucked me into it the first time. If it hadn't been for the amazing breakthrough that came with it, I would dismiss the idea out of hand. Do me a favor and go over there," said Laurenz, pointing to a remote corner of the lab. "Go dormant while I discuss it with my colleagues."

Again, Laurenz had to endure Alaurenz's sardonic expression and unsaid comment. Alaurenz turned to go. When he was out of earshot, Laurenz barked at his mute assistants. "He thinks it's funny. The holo-bastard knows he has us captive of a revolutionary discovery, and he can close the door anytime. After all, it takes cooperation of both worlds to make the contact. I'm sure our motivations are the same in regards to the science involved, but as of now the main reason we were persuaded to go there is because of the trouble they are in. What do you think we should do?"

"Well . . . there doesn't seem to be any danger in it," said Nate. "In some ways, it is even better than one of those Disneyland adventures. You are not only close to the action, but you can participate in it without getting hurt."

"For us, perhaps so, but in other ways no," said Laurenz. "Real lives are at stake. And when I engaged that character in the coffee shop, it was real, just as it was when I witnessed the Cleansing Reductions at the cathedral. There was no physical discomfort involved, but the psychic stress was the same as if I had actually been there."

"Maybe . . . it would be better to go with someone," said Sye, who had remained quiet during the exchange.

A moment's silence followed before Laurenz took it up. "And what would be the advantage of that?"

"Several things," said Sye slowly. "Something familiar is always comforting and stress relieving. A second person could provide support in any tasks Alaurenz might have in mind and, frankly, could watch your back."

"There's nobody who can go," said Laurenz. "You guys need to stay here and mind the equipment and secure the conditions for my transfer. We don't want someone blundering in here during the process, and we certainly can't go outside the project for someone. As of now, there are none but us three, Marcia, and Christian who have the slightest idea how far the project has progressed. The university oversight knows only that we are making soundings through devices associated with known theory. If we weren't funded by the UMC, we would have been cancelled long ago. Most of my colleagues laugh at us anyway, but because of the grant, they are envious."

"How about Christian?" asked Nate.

"Well, he . . . Christian? I don't know if that would be such a good idea," offered Laurenz in anemic dissent at the same time searching through a compendium of vague fears for more solid reasons. "Besides, Marcia might not go for it."

"But why not?" said Nate. "It would be like Batman and Robin."

"Funny, very funny. Still, if I could convince Marcia that there would be no danger, she might agree. No use asking Christian. He would jump at the chance. Let's get together, and I will bring up the subject with Marcia in private." said Laurenz. "Let me go and get Alaurenz."

He passed down to the dim nook where Alaurenz stood shimmering. *Look at that*, thought Laurenz. *I didn't glow like that on Otherearth.* His face held that same pointed expression as before. "Come back and talk to us," said Laurenz with forced geniality. "By the way, why do you have that aura around your image? I didn't have that when I visited your world."

"It is the interaction with trace elements in your atmosphere. We designed the polymeric fill to fit the characteristics of our own, which is similar but minutely different enough to cause the effect you observe."

"Sorry I asked," said Laurenz.

They passed back to where Sye and Nate stood. "We have decided to help you," said Laurenz. "The breakthrough we have made is too important to scuttle because of problems in one of our worlds. I have to confess that when it is known here that another world not only exists but can be contacted, all hell is going to break loose. Thank goodness aggression and conquest are impossible between our worlds given what we know now about transfer." *That is, I think it is,* thought Laurenz, suddenly aware of the catastrophic implications of the other-world probe running amuck.

"My colleagues have suggested that I not go alone," continued Laurenz, momentarily disheveled by the intruding thought. "A young associate may be recruited to go with me if it meets your approval."

"It does," said Alaurenz cryptically.

"Good. It will take us a few days to fabricate another seclusion chamber and make other . . . uh, arrangements. In the meantime, you can either stay here or deactivate your hologram and tend to pressing matters on Otherearth."

"Thank you. Things are uncertain there, so I will retire to an out-of-the-way corner of your laboratory and do the latter. I will deactivate and trust that you will discard my fill and dispose of it."

Alaurenz again moved to the dim recesses of the lab and was suddenly still, the faint iridescence still emanating from his form.

XIV

"Of course I would like to go, whatever that means," choked an exuberant Christian in answer to Laurenz' casual probe.

"You understand I must okay this with Marcia," Laurenz noted. "She is your senior and, unofficially at least, your protector and overseer and answerable to the family while you are here."

"Of course, but if she decides to present it to my father, how will she do it without revealing the true nature of your work? And would he even understand it if she decided to do so?" said Christian.

"You are right there," said Laurenz with a pause. "We are so far out that even our colleagues in the scientific community would have trouble with it. I will just have to pass it by her and see how she reacts."

Laurenz decided a romantic outing would be the best place to broach the subject. He picked up Marcia at the dorm, and they drove to a favorite on the lakeshore.

"I am going to order a scotch on the rocks," said Laurenz. "How about you?"

"I will have a tequila Collins."

The drinks arrived; Laurenz took a dainty sip, while Marcia demolished half hers in one gulp. *Good,* he thought, *maybe it will loosen her up.* He studied the object of his affection, waiting for inspiration as just how to bring up the subject. He was about to plunge ahead when Marcia spoke.

"So anything happen at the lab today?"

"Yes. Alaurenz showed up again."

"That's great," said Marcia unexpectedly.

Taking the lead, Laurenz responded. "I take it you have warmed to the idea of an other-world visitor."

"I think it is the coolest thing that has happened in this humdrum world and in this staid academic setting in particular," said Marcia.

"Cool, that's what Christian said it was," said Laurenz casually. "I wonder how the idea of Christian going back to Otherearth with me would strike you."

Marcia was silent for a moment. "Well now, I will just have to think about that." Apparently the drink had not dulled her senses or compromised her judgment.

"You know he will be secluded and perfectly safe here. It shouldn't disrupt his studies since he is only taking a light load of classes till fall, and his real-time exposure to Otherearth will be the same as here because his sleep-rest cycle corresponds to the day-night cycle there."

"Whose bright idea was it?" asked Marcia.

"Nate and Sye's. They thought two might equal three in this situation, if you get my drift."

"Let me think about it," said Marcia.

They dined and immersed themselves in intimacy and small talk, but Laurenz could see Marcia had turned serious and was preoccupied with the issue of Christian's involvement in the other-world project.

A day later, Marcia showed up at the lab.

"What if I went too?" she asked.

Caught unaware, Laurenz stammered mutilated and unconvincing versions of the clichés "two's company" and "too many cooks" and opted for a limp complication. "What about your classes?"

"We are near summer break. I am sure I can do it."

It was not a good idea to start with, or it was and won't work out, thought Laurenz. "I think I should go back alone and deal with the situation as well as possible. After all, this is a scientific breakthrough that we must foster and savor. We have to take it slowly, minimize our involvement in the affairs of the target world, and hopefully maintain our contact."

"Well, I am warming to the idea," said Marcia. "Let's talk more about it. You will have to make another of those . . . chambers."

Laurenz was standing beside one of the transfer chambers briefing an eager Christian and taciturn Marcia.

"Remember, after you transfer, from your standpoint your hologram will think it is just between two mirrors as the origin of the reflection. You will see yourself repeated as far as the seventh reflection where you made entry into Otherearth. Move laterally, and you will complete the transition. I will go first and be waiting."

"Got it," said Christian. "When do we go?"

"We can go when Nate and Sye are ready. It will take them another day or so to finish the other chambers and headpieces. Then—"

The buzzer sounded, indicating that they had a visitor. Laurenz leaned over to scrutinize the video monitor. *Freda, Christ.*

"Freda! What a surprise. Wait a moment, and I will buzz you in."

"Who is that?" asked Marcia.

"Freda Freeland, big wheel in the UMC and the liaison to their reach into the real world."

"What does she want?"

"Well, I guess two things," said Laurenz pensively, as if considering it for the first time, "To know just where their money is going and, in harmony with their worldview, to use us to achieve a link to the transcendent spiritual unknown. You guys make yourselves scarce while I deal with her."

The group drifted to as inconspicuous a point that the tight confines of the lab would permit as Freda floated across the floor toward Laurenz, her long dress concealing the short, quick movements of her legs.

"Hello, Laurenz. I felt I should stop by to tell you that we are doing a routine review of our budget and expenditures. I am in there as a strong supporter of your work but felt that if I could give them something a little more tangible than the exciting, though somewhat abstract description of your advances, I could then be more of a convincing advocate."

This is going to be tricky, thought Laurenz. "As a matter of fact, I was just about to call you. Thanks to your generous support, we have moved forward from the primitive contact I reported on your last visit. Unfortunately, we have thus far been unable to commune with the dead, but it is now possible to transfer our . . . spirit—that is, the essence of ourselves—to another world similar in many respects to ours. I myself have made this journey and report what may be a disappointment to you that it is deficient in even more ways than our own in its embrace of spiritual values." *That should hold her for a bit.*

"This is wonderful. It is what we have all wished for. When can I go?"

She has heard only the part she wanted to hear. "Uh . . . well, like I have said, it is not the place you may have imagined—that is, the . . . the Olympus of divine presence or the Valhalla of the enlightened. I think you would find it possesses significant deficiencies short of your expectations."

"Then . . . if it was hardly worth the effort we have expended to accomplish it, perhaps we should—"

"Oh I . . . I think you will find in the . . . journey, the out-of-body experience itself, a process of rebirth, transforming, and satisfying enough," stammered Laurenz, leaping to the rescue.

"That's just marvelous. Then I take it you can arrange for me to go?"

"There was never any doubt," soothed Laurenz in a low-pitched monotone.

"I must hurry back to the Coalition headquarters with the news."

"Perhaps we should, for now, keep the mission secret," cautioned Laurenz. "By no means would I wish to indefinitely deprive your members of this profound breakthrough to the spiritual other-land, but there are forces in our society who do not share our belief, not to mention our enthusiasm, for this effort."

"I see what you mean. I will only disclose it to the executive board and look forward to a full exposition of the experience when it is done," said Freda, wafting toward the door.

The exiled group slowly gathered around Laurenz and stood quietly.

"Don't say a word," he growled as the lab was suddenly filled with peals of laughter. "You must have heard it all."

"We do have to hand it to you. Such vision, such finesse," sang Marcia.

"Shut up."

"Do you actually intend to send her?" asked Nate.

"I may have no choice. You heard me trash Otherearth. She didn't even hear it," said Laurenz. "In any case, we should prepare another chamber."

In spite of heroic efforts, Laurenz was unable to dissuade Freda from the odyssey that would define her purpose in life. All was made ready. Freda, Marcia, Christian, and Laurenz were trussed up in their couches with the brain function sensors in place. Nate was studying the control panel a few steps away. "I can energize it anytime. Everything checks out."

"As we planned, you will transfer me first and then the others in quick succession," said Laurenz.

"Got it."

Laurenz emerged from the mirror space to chaos. Sounds of pounding and voices came from the outside. The lab personnel were surging about, some setting equipment for self-destruct, while others were making for prearranged escape routes.

Alaurenz shouted from across the lab floor as he ran towards Laurenz. "It happened just as we had indication that you were coming through. The Guardians are on to us. They may have traced our signals through leakage in the transmitter."

Laurenz' instincts took over. "Don't shut down just now, give it a few seconds. More are coming through. We don't know what damage to the primary can be caused by aborting the transfer in the middle of it. How long do we have?"

"No time. We don't even have time to destroy the equipment. The others must arrive soon or—"

"Here they are," said Laurenz as Christian's, Marcia's, and Freda's holograms stepped out of the gap between the mirrors in succession.

Laurenz snapped, "Which way?"

"Follow me," said Alaurenz as he did a quick up and down of the group. "They are using explosives to destroy the row of fail-safe doors we have used as a barrier."

"Where are we going? What's happening?" asked Christian and Marcia in overlapping queries.

"Oh dear," said Freda.

"The local authorities have discovered the operation here," said Alaurenz. "We must get away as quickly as possible. Your forms still have no solidity, and we need to go to our standby facility to do this. You are conspicuous in your present form. Close inspection or physical encounter with anyone would reveal your true nature and raise questions."

With Alaurenz' urging, the five of them made for a back corner of the work space. Alaurenz opened a paneled section of the wall, closing and sealing it as they passed through. A spiral staircase led downward. As they reached the bottom, a long, dimly lighted passage stretched before them. It took several minutes to tread its length, but they finally emerged in a vast underground tunnel extending in both directions. To the left was unknown darkness, but to the right in the distance was a vaulted opening to the outside. They edged along beside the shallow stream of water that ran down the middle of the passageway as they moved toward the light.

Christian looked around. "The signals controlling us seem to go through anything, like neutrinos."

"It's a completely different thing," said Laurenz. "When other dimensions enter the picture, distance, intervening matter, and even temporal issues are apparently irrelevant."

Emerging from the tunnel, they entered an open channel with an occasional stairway leading upward. Alaurenz chose one, and they made their way up and out into a residential neighborhood.

"That was a satellite duct leading to the main drainage system that flows through Braddock on the south side of the city and terminates in the river," said Alaurenz, gesturing behind. "Now we must avoid close scrutiny with any of the people and detour if such seems inevitable."

"If I had known we were going for a hike, I would have worn different shoes," groused Marcia, knowing that neither the light loafers she wore nor the unscheduled trek presented discomfort because of her edited senses.

"How far is the other lab?" asked Laurenz.

"Some distance away on foot, in the warehouse district on the periphery of the city," said Alaurenz. "It is our main base, more secure but somewhat remote from the center of action, which is the reason we were operating from the site in Old Town."

Freda, though in her holographic form still appeared clad in her retro outfit, was moved to comment. "This is not quite what I expected. We could as well be back home, and I am not entirely convinced that we are not. Are you sure we have entered another plane of existence?"

"Yes," said Laurenz on the edge of his patience. "The similarity you allude to is precisely why we were able to come here. It is related to the science involved. You will find, in due course, significant differences between here and where we came from. The violence you witnessed on arrival should have given you a hint."

They passed from the center of the city to the fringes, the landscape now ever more dominated by industrial-type buildings. Alaurenz finally stopped in front of one of these. The ill-kept doorway signaled some sort of gruff, low-tech activity within. He pushed the door open, and they entered. A large machine dominated the floor area. Nobody was in sight, but the machine hummed and churned as if it had just been abandoned for some reason.

Nobody around, thought Laurenz. *I guess they are all on a break. I wonder what they make here. Oh—those plastic containers. The raw materials enter over there.*

"It's our cover," said Alaurenz. "At a moment's notice, the crew whom we will meet presently can take up positions in the production line of this everyday product. We have false inventory, orders, and production schedules ready for inspection should anyone ask."

Alaurenz led them to a shadowy back corner. A row of dust-covered production rejects were stacked against the wall flanked by a bank of unkempt lockers. Alaurenz placed his palm a spot on the adjacent wall, and four of the lockers swung easily outward. They entered a well-lighted area strewn with equipment. "Only a skeleton crew is here now, as the others who were at the Old Town facility are regrouping and, according to prearranged plans, will reconvene here. In the meantime we must add solidity to your holograms and wait for Allfather Bakel, our insider, to coordinate a plan of action. By now, he has undoubtedly heard about the raid on the Old Town lab."

XV

"They didn't capture anyone?" said Verkezian.

"No," said Ganderk. "They all escaped. And there is some mystery about the source controlling the hologram. The signal peaked just as we were entering the hidden lab. It appears that the equipment had been set to destruct, but our intervention was so quick that some of it is still intact. Romarda says the technicians can use the method they used to produce the proxy and can reconstruct the machine and instruments from the remnants, as well as determine where his real counterpart resides. He is also scrutinizing an odd assortment of mirrors that were concentrated at the center of the instrumentation and whose purpose is unknown."

"Keep me informed. I must convene the Council."

Archfather Verkezian rose and spoke gravely. "It is as we feared. A cell of dissidents has managed to operate undetected until now. The Guardians have discovered this lair of sinners and neutralized it. Unfortunately, no captives were taken, and no specimens of the strange proxies mentioned in our last meeting were found."

Allfather Bakel, who stood listening, was moved to ask, "Do you think that is the end of it?"

"Obviously not," said Verkezian. "They will set up somewhere else if they haven't already."

"They are too few to cause us trouble, whatever plans they may have for disruption," said Allfather Leeche.

"Not so," said Allfather Corvus. "The Congregation is like a house of cards. Any breach of our control, and the flock will rise against us. We must exercise increased vigil, especially regarding the suppression broadcasts."

Allfather Bakel joined in as many throughout the Council murmured assent.

"Before we go forward, I would like to hear from Adjunctfather Romarda concerning any findings of relevance by the DDS," said Verkezian.

"Yes," replied Romarda. "We have ambiguous findings concerning the origin and nature of the controlling signal. Most puzzling is that the signal persists even though the instruments that facilitated it are either destroyed or no longer functioning, which leads us to conclude that although it came from there, there is no evidence that it originated there."

In a coordinated blink, those assembled stared at Romarda to fathom what he had just said.

"You are saying that it came from there, but it didn't," said Allfather Corvus sarcastically. "What in the name of His Divine Presence does that mean?"

"You will pardon me for making a muddle of it," said Romarda.

"But . . . since you traced the signal to the place where you originally thought it was coming from, can you not now focus in on the place it originates or is being relayed from?" uttered an exasperated Corvus.

Romarda answered with a hesitant, "No. That is, maybe. The source is not on this planet. Evidence shows that it was relayed from another source located somewhere else. There are no directional vectors to other places on Earth, and most disturbing, there are none pointing . . . well, up, to some extraterrestrial source. The central conundrum is that the source disappears, which said another way, it seems to come from nowhere. Once established, it persists indefinitely as long as there exist conditions for it to do so. This suggests that there may be similar facilities in other places."

Romarda could see the frustration on the faces of the Council. *Should I leave it there or go further?* he thought. With a sigh, he continued. "The resistance has perhaps found some way to tap other dimensions or alternate worlds. They could be using it for subversive purposes. The array of mirrors we found may give us a lead, as it has been posited in scientific literature that such might be used to interact with a parallel world."

An unhinged Archfather Verkezian blurted out. "Such things or even thoughts of them are forbidden by canon law. They render askew the Oneness of our world and the unique place we have in the universe."

"Your Highness, I have just told you the facts and possibilities as they are revealed to us through the scientific method," replied a subdued Romarda. "We do not vouch for the ultimate truth of them. I had hoped the issue would not arise, but events have forced it to the surface. It must be pointed out that there is a conflict between our mandate of loyalty to the Church and that which it requires us to do true science. Further, and without disputing church doctrine, I would remind the holy fathers here assembled that all the scientific thought leading to the technology used to control the populace, as well as that which has led to the growth of modern civilization, were once viewed as heresy."

"We have reconciled them with church doctrine," snapped Verkezian, hesitant to pursue the matter.

The moment of silence that descended over the Council was finally broken by the grate of Allfather Corvus's voice. "To hell with the niceties of doctrine. We must do all to counter the insurgency. I say authorize the DDS to pursue the leads suggesting other . . . realms of existence and report back to us."

The assembly sat tense but passive, listening to the dialogue between Verkezian, Romarda, and Corvus.

I should have expected it, thought Bakel. *Romarda is just an inch from becoming one of us. He knows that his precious science cannot flourish in a world of religious restriction. A slight nudge could bring him over, if he was not so humbled and enmeshed in the culture of the Congregation.*

Alaurenz' phone rang, and the voice said, "Mr. Kapro, I must speak to you about a change in the order I made this morning."

"Certainly, anytime at the office."

"I'll be there this afternoon."

"That was Bakel," said Alaurenz. "It must be important, or he would not have taken the risk of calling."

Part of the crew had reassembled, and all focused on the security monitor, as Allfather Bakel could be seen entering the vast outer area of the pseudo factory. He nodded at the camera hidden in the darkened truss area of the roof and passed through the opening that appeared as the locker door swung back.

"They may have figured out what you are doing," said Bakel. "Romarda has reported to them the enigmas surrounding the controlling source of holograms. I was not sure how it worked myself, as you have not explained it, but they are on the fundamental idea that the analogs are being controlled from a point that is not of the world we inhabit."

"That is quite a leap in intuition," said Alaurenz. "I am impressed that they have gone that far, but it leaves us with latitude, because they still will not be able to figure out how we do it."

"Don't bet on it," said Bakel. "Romarda is no slouch as a scientist. He mentioned research involving the mirror arrangement they found in Old Town and something about parallel worlds. I have a feeling they are into things at the DDS that fall well outside that permitted by the church. Science tends to pull one inexorably into areas of dark and gray. One thing is for sure, he is fatally timid. He would not defy the Congregation but would come over to us if a coup were successful."

"All right, but now we must go forward," said Alaurenz. "I would like for you to do this for me. The young man you met last time, Cralle, lives over near Braddock. Here is his address. Go there and warn him not to go near the old lab. He and Janize, whom you also met, probably do not know of its demise. Tell him of our present location and ask him to come here. He is trained in electronics. If you can use your influence to get him and Laurenz in the DDS, we can employ the combined the virtues of both to the execution of the plan."

"The plan being?"

"To neutralize the suppression broadcasts and put them out of action long enough for an insurrection to gain momentum."

"All right, I'm willing to take the chance. Each of the Allfathers on the Council can recommend to positions in the limitless bureaucracy of the Congregation, the DDS being one of them. It's one of the perks. But we are responsible for their conduct. If any overt subversion is linked to Cralle and the Holo, I can be called to task—or worse."

"Understood," Alaurenz noted. "We will be prepared to take you underground if necessary."

Cralle opened his door to reveal the priest whom he had met in the lab. "Allfather Bakel! You gave me a start like the first time I saw you."

"Sorry about that, but get over it. Things are moving fast and furious. Alaurenz has dispatched me to inform you that the lab you visited has been discovered and destroyed. The alternate facility is more remote, and I am here to tell you of its location and inform you in advance of the plan. If you are willing, I will insert you in the DDS if possible along with another whose aspect you will discover at the proper time."

Cralle gave Bakel a long look and shrugged. "Whatever you have in mind, I am ready and anxious to meet my mysterious coconspirator."

"Our aim is to penetrate the interior of the Breath of God facility, the source of the suppression broadcasts. Now here—take this crude map. It has marked on it the remote lab. The location is a modest manufactory and is the front for our clandestine operation. Commit it to memory and then destroy it."

Cralle stood in front of the innocuous industrial building. Rechecking the faded number on the facade, he shrugged and tried the door. It resisted at first but gave way as he heard a click that signaled he had been cleared to pass in. His attention first fell on the solitary machine that dominated the floor, but a movement in the recesses of the enclosure told him that his new allies were expecting him.

"Glad you decided to help us," said Alaurenz.

"Allfather Bakel didn't have to do much persuading," said Cralle.

"Come back inside our main facility here, and I will explain our plan."

Cralle followed Alaurenz back through the locker door to where Laurenz and the others stood waiting. Cralle gaped at one of the figures as he came closer. "This—is your brother? He is the one who intervened at the coffee house. I thought there was something familiar about you when we first met back there, but I put it on hold in the anxiety of the moment."

"Not exactly my brother," said Alaurenz. "I will tell you right off that he and the others here are not real, but holographic representations of real persons. Perhaps more jolting to common sense is that he is my counterpart from a parallel world who, by our mutual efforts, has come here."

Cralle, seldom at a loss for words, finally found his voice. "I had no idea that such a thing existed or was possible and am amazed that you have moved this far in leading edge science amid the strictures imposed by the Congregation."

"We had been striving for interworld contact long before the Congregation's grip was absolute," said Alaurenz. "Now, if Bakel can maneuver you and Laurenz here into the DDS's Breath of God facility, we will try to disable the suppression transmission. That done, we will have a limited time window for the liberated populace to generate a mass movement to displace the leadership. We have no desire to abolish the church, only to purge the perverse dictatorial elements within it. We may, however, consider destroying the temple itself, which has become a symbol of the Congregation's degradation and tyranny. To fill the power vacuum, we will enlist the latent opposition within the Church to steer it back to a proportionate place in the scheme of things. We aim to restore a secular government by freeing those of the former political parties who have survived Cleansing and are still in prison. From there, they can fight it out as to who is in charge."

"No offence," said Cralle with a nod toward Laurenz. "But what is the advantage of including a . . . a virtual person in this mission, especially one who is a stranger to our world?"

"He cannot be harmed," said Alaurenz. "With no bodily needs, he can go dormant in a secluded place indefinitely and emerge at an optimum time, or disengage entirely from his proxy. The only considerations are the corporal needs of his dormant body back on the parallel Earth he came from and the stress of action here. Also, Laurenz is a scientist back there, not a warrior, although his performance in the coffee shop should leave no reservations as to his courage. Also, we have paired you two because he will need a partner who understands behavior and protocols of our world and can assist in any scientific endeavor."

"This young man, Christian, where do he and the two young ladies fit in?" asked Cralle.

"Christian is my support and backup, and this is Marcia, sister to Christian," said Laurenz injecting himself into the exchange for the first time. "She is part of the mission, and Ms. Freda Freeland, she uh . . . has a profound interest in the success of our interworld contact since the organization she represents funds the effort on our end."

That should satisfy both, thought Laurenz.

Alaurenz surveyed the disparate group with mixed feelings. *I guess it is to be expected that our visitors would not take as seriously as we do our situation here. I just hope they don't get in the way.* "All right, the advantage you bring to our struggle is invaluable, and I would like to use it to the maximum, which means to attack the Congregation's grip on several fronts. In addition to the mission I have outlined for Laurenz and Cralle, we need to expose the abject aspects of the Congregation hierarchy, which is deeper than you can imagine. A pathetic segment of Allfathers and sub clergy have recruited a harem of younger girls and boys to act as sex slaves. We have dubbed them the Licentia.

"Oh my goodness," murmured Freda, who until then had been only passively monitoring the exchange.

"Once selected, they ramp up the suppression on the victim and inform any of the victim's relatives that they have been recruited into the service of the Church," continued Alaurenz. "According to Allfather Bakel, they do this by selectively targeting choice candidates from a hidden observation perch at the temple during the forced visits to the temple. Prime candidates are unaccompanied post adolescents from, say, fifteen to twenty-five, but other victims are chosen at the whim or taste of the Licentia. If they have no ties or are orphaned, it's even better. The Council looks the other way.

"We need an inside operative to make a record of the goings on and were thinking about asking your companion Janize to do it for us. Now that Christian has showed up, we may be able to use him as backup and, perhaps, bait also. If we can get one or both in, we can monitor the goings on, get names and photos, and expose the whole den of iniquity. Even though she is free of the suppression, Janize will be the most vulnerable, because Christian cannot be harmed."

"But wouldn't they eventually have to . . . that is, perform and, in doing so or refusing to, as in the case of Christian, reveal themselves?" asked Laurenz.

"We think they can get in and out before that happens, since we will time it with the diversion of an assault on the Breath of God broadcast facility."

"Wait a minute. I witnessed her narrow miss the first time," said Laurenz. "The same joker who first intercepted her or even the goon in the coffee shop may recognize her."

"We can alter her appearance enough to get her in the temple unrecognized," said Alaurenz. "Besides, none of the Licentia were witness to the altercation involving her. We think we can get them in and out before they realize what is going on."

"Okay, they can't harm Christian, but the girl is still in danger," said Laurenz. "You will be taking a chance with her."

"Along with a device to record the perverse activities, we will give her a weapon for emergencies," said Alaurenz.

Cralle, who had been taking it in, also expressed reservations. "It seems too dangerous to me. What if things go wrong?"

Alaurenz' frustration surfaced. "We need a diversion and then coordinated action on several fronts to confuse and overwhelm the Congregation. Some chances have to be taken. If we can persuade Janize to do it, okay; if not, it's still okay."

"So when do we start?" asked Cralle, giving in to Alaurenz' plan.

"Now," said Alaurenz. "Take Christian and talk to Janize and then come back here and spend the night. Bakel is making arrangements so that you and Laurenz will meet him at the DDS Administration Building tomorrow. In the meantime, Laurenz and Marcia can go dormant and take care of commitments and bodily needs back on their world."

"Okay," said Cralle finally. "I'll take Christian and talk to her."

"I'll go too," said Marcia.

"Marcia," said Laurenz in low tones as he moved closer. "We have a problem. What do we do with?" He indicated Freda with the flick of the head. "Could you possibly babysit her while we get on with the plan? You have seen what this world is like now, more or less like ours. Christian will be all right," he added not quite convinced that the unexpected could not happen.

"What on earth would I do with her?"

"Well, go into the city and see the sights. She will probably flip when she starts soaking up the many differences from our world. Just stay clear of the Guardians. They stand out, because they are usually dressed in black and stand around as if they have nothing else to do. When you get tired, come back with her and go dormant. Both of you will need some rest and food back on Earth. You can return tomorrow for another tourist trek."

"Okay," said Marcia with hesitation. "I guess my vague fears were exaggerated back on Earth. The place doesn't seem as ominous as when you had originally described it."

A knock brought Janize to her door. A cautious look through the peep hole showed Cralle and shoulder of someone else just out of sight. She opened the door to face Cralle and another about her same age.

"Janize, this is Christian," said Cralle in haste to explain the presence of a stranger. "Alaurenz has sent us both with a request that you help us in a coordinated attack on the Congregation, but first I must explain something about my friend Christian. He is not a real person. For this reason, we think he is the perfect vehicle for the mission we have in mind. He—"

"He's not what?" asked a perplexed Janize, whose eyes had never left the handsome Christian.

How can I explain this thing to which the senses rebel, thought Cralle. *And should I bring up the subject of where his primary actually is?* "He is a product of a new science that can take the physical and cognitive aspects of someone and place them in a three-dimensional representation. The real person he represents is . . . elsewhere."

"So he's real, just not here," said Janize with a tinge of sarcasm. Though skeptical, she was relieved and scarcely unhinged at the thought of it.

"Well, yes," said Cralle. "Now, if you are up to it, here's what Alaurenz would like for you to do."

Janize listened intensely as Cralle explained the broad assault on the Congregation. It suddenly dawned on her that her first aborted encounter with the Guardians may have ended with her in an Allfather harem.

"Where does Christian come in?" asked Janize.

"He is also bait but will be a backup in case of trouble," said Cralle. "His virtual form gives us an advantage in that he cannot be harmed. Whichever role he plays depends on chance and the actions of the Licentia, which is what Alaurenz' group calls them. You will be provided with a weapon should things get out of control. Oh—and wear something skimpy."

"When do we do this?" asked Janize.

"It will be a diversion and immediately prior to other action to nullify the suppression broadcasts," said Cralle. "I would ask if he could stay here till the action is called for. You can put him in a closet, and he can go dormant until you are instructed to move."

"But would he just stay there?"

"Only his shell."

"How will he know the proper time? And, come to think of it, where is the person he actually represents?" asked Janize, the bizarre aspects of Christian's form only now soaking in.

Cralle settled for, "He will re inhabit the hologram periodically and check in with you. His actual self is in a place that cannot be reached."

Janize did a slow take, focusing first on Christian then Cralle. Alright, Christian, come over here," she said, taking him by the arm and leading him to a closet. "And knock before you open the door if you decide to come out."

She stood looking at him before closing the door and said to Cralle without turning, "Does he talk?"

"Hi," said Christian with a grin.

Janize met Christian's bratty affront with a cold stare and an assertive slam of the door. She turned to Cralle. "You are sure he will behave himself while in there?"

"I am sure, because most of the time he won't even be there."

XVI

Bakel waited a few blocks from the Breath of God facility. The sprinkling of passersby flowed easily, giving the morning job commute a feeling of normality. No extraordinary Guardian presence was apparent. He spied Laurenz and Cralle rounding a corner and advanced to meet them.

"Let me do the talking. The Allfathers are pushing for favors within the bureaucracy all the time, so we shouldn't expect anything but routine grumbling from the personnel officer. Cralle, you are okay as far as background is concerned, but I had to fake some credentials for Laurenz."

They approached the DDS headquarters, a tapering edifice thinning as it rose and topped out with a large statue of the savior, sloping to a broad base. From what they could see, the ground floor had been completely leased to small commercial shops, belying its sinister purpose. Only the guarded entrance at its center suggested its main function.

"Its outer appearance is deceptive," said Bakel. "It extends far underground where is located the power and backup for the intricate supporting machinery, the instrumentation above that transmits the controlling signal, and the cables sending the suppression signals to the extremities of the nation. That would be the target of last resort since below the second level all is unknown except to the higher ranks of the Congregation and the staff who mans it. You would be going in blind. More vulnerable is the antenna on the roof."

"Where, I don't see any antenna," said Cralle.

"It is masked by the shell of the savior's statue," said Bakel.

"To disable it we will have to destroy the statue," said Laurenz.

"If you must, you must," said Bakel. "The savior is now being dishonored by the evil things being done in his name."

They entered the building and passed the first layer of security as Bakel signed the ledger for himself and the two visitors. A bored officer questioned Laurenz and Cralle and assigned them to the electronic maintenance division with low clearance, while an approving Allfather Bakel looked on.

"I'm sure the families of these men will be proud to know that they are on track to do service for the Church," oozed Bakel to the noncommittal grunt of the personnel officer.

Bakel left Cralle and Laurenz to their resources with the quiet admonishment,

"Until you can act decisively, try not to exceed the limits of your permitted status here, since I am answerable for it. But find out as much as you can about the central mechanism of the suppression transmitter, its location, and its vulnerabilities."

Laurenz and Cralle were taken to a brief orientation along with a few others and placed under the supervision of one of the technicians, who appeared to be connected to the clergy based on his dress. The V in the front of a charcoal-colored jumpsuit framed a white shirt and black tie. A golden chain disappeared into the bowels of the suit from which undoubtedly hung the inverted crucifix.

Left alone a few moments, Cralle observed, "The DDS is relatively secular, so it looks like the Congregation has planted a cadre of midlevel clergy to watch over their bosses and any suspect activity."

The technician conducted them to the maintenance division and assigned each a work station. "Recalibrate and then test those relay transmitters and make a report. You will work until five with an hour for lunch." He walked away, leaving Cralle and Laurenz alone.

"These are more or less straight forward," said Cralle. "They pick up and boost the suppression signal from the central transmitting center. We hope to find out where that is in this labyrinth, although our degree of clearance would not allow us to penetrate it—officially, that is."

Laurenz considered. "There may be another approach. How much is the dissemination of the signal dependent on the relays?"

"For complete, no-holes coverage, a lot," said Cralle. "Terrain, structures, and other natural and manmade features attenuate, or sometimes completely nullify, the suppression signal, even though they have taken pains to plug the gaps. Original surveys pinpointed the areas, and the relays were strategically placed to assure blanket coverage. They can also be manipulated remotely to ramp up or diminish the signal strength in any locality."

"Maybe they can be manipulated to do the opposite," said Laurenz. "Then we wouldn't have to sabotage the BOG transmission at its origin."

"I see what you are getting at," said Cralle. "We can analyze the circuitry and devise a countersignal to freeze or scramble the broadcast, and we are in an ideal place to do it here in maintenance. There is plenty of miscellaneous hardware around we can use. Let's get to it and fix the lame ones here on the bench. They are probably all suffering from a similar malfunction. Then we can use one of the functioning ones to experiment on."

"I will depend on you for the right approach," said Laurenz. "These transmissions use customized frequencies in the electromagnetic spectrum that act directly in the brain not unlike the process that controls me now. Alaurenz showed us how to generate them, but due to time constraints, he never explained the underlying theory."

"You can dig into the theory later, but in general, your guess is right," said Cralle. "The difference is that the

Congregation's transmission is omnidirectional and targeted for a single function in the brain, that which controls initiative and aggression. For now, what we need to do is concentrate on neutralizing the signal."

"Right. If you can get a hook on it before quitting time, we can start putting together the attenuator tomorrow in our spare time."

The day ended, and Laurenz and Cralle returned to the lab.

Christian rose from the recliner, removed the helmet sensor, and emerged from the chamber. Only Sye was there.

"What's going on? Laurenz is still in the chamber."

"He is still occupied, and I have been given an assignment that will require my reappearance at a specific time," said Christian. "For now, I need to get some food, exercise, and rest. I'll be back here in the morning."

He passed the evening catching up on some of the studies he had fallen behind on and then flopped onto his dorm couch for some moments of rest.

Sun streamed through the window, rousing Christian with a jolt. *Christ, I must have overslept*, he thought. He slipped on some clothes, grabbed some breakfast he could consume on the way, and made for the lab. Everybody was there. Laurenz had emerged from his chamber just after Christian the previous night. Marcia and Freda returned several hours later when Marcia had finally corralled the wayward hippie and returned to the lab.

"I thought I needed a breather before going back," said Laurenz.

"Me too," said Christian. "I didn't realize how stressful it would be over there. I'm sure it's the idea of it—the newness and the experience of something that is both familiar and unfamiliar."

"I see it affects someone else like that," said Laurenz. "I thought I was indulging myself when events weighed so heavily on me after the first trip. So where are you with the girl and Alaurenz's plan?"

"I am in a state of dormancy in a closet in her apartment," said Christian with a hint of mischief.

"You better get back there pronto and get on with it," said Laurenz. "We need to wind this thing up so that we can concentrate on science. I will follow, as Cralle and I need to be at 'work' by 9:00 a.m. I am thankful the time on Otherearth runs in tandem with ours so that our internal clocks won't have to adjust every time we make the hop."

"How about us?" asked Marcia indicating herself and Freda.

Damn, double damn, thought Laurenz, eyeing his love of life. *Marcia, I haven't been able to concentrate on her, us. When this is over, the both of us are taking a long vacation.*

"If you are refreshed enough, go when we go," said Laurenz with a sigh.

Janize jumped out of her wits when she heard the knocking from inside her closet door. In her early morning stupor, she had almost forgotten her bizarre roommate as she staggered to her coffee maker and barked, "Don't come out yet! I'm not dressed. Christian waited patiently and could hear Janize rummaging around. She finally opened the door, and he sauntered out.

"Morning," he sang.

"Good morning. Next time knock softer," she snapped. "Could I offer you some . . . can you eat?

"Yes and no," replied Christian. "In this form no, but back home I ate before transferring."

"I'm famished. I hope you don't mind if I have some breakfast," she said politely.

"Go ahead, I'll just sit here and stare," said Christian.

In her early morning haze, something annoyed Janize as she gazed at Christian. She looked him up and down. "And just what are you going to stare at?"

"You," said Christian without a pause.

"And why should you do that?"

"Because you are very pretty even at this hour and have a spicy attitude, which I find fetching."

A disarmed Janize blushed and turned to her modest repast with an occasional sideways glance at the handsome Christian who stood immobile. She finished and began to clear away the dishes.

"Janize, we need to go to the main facility," said Christian. "The rest of us otherworlders should be there now, and Alaurenz has plans for us."

"Okay, give me a second. Otherworlders, what does that mean?"

"Oh, that's right. Cralle was not very specific about where I came from. My companions and I are based on another world similar to this one. Alaurenz, along with parallel efforts from us, has devised a way for our proxies to move from one to another."

Janize stopped her cleanup and stared at Christian. "Let me understand what you are saying. Just where is this world? Is it another country or continent?"

"No, something entirely different. It is hard to explain," said Christian. "I don't entirely understand it myself, but the place I am from runs parallel to this world and is as real as it is here."

"And parallel means what?" asked a perplexed Janize.

"Think of it as another Earth, existing somewhere, just like it is here in general but differing in detail. The where cannot be answered in terms of position or how far, only in terms of advanced understanding of the true nature of our existence through science."

"I think we will let it rest for now," said Janize, warming to the precocious but intelligent Christian.

One by one they transferred with each re-inhabiting his polymeric shell. Marcia tested her fill. As she pressed hard, she could feel pressure but no hint of discomfort. *The holoform filters out pain and discomfort but not tactile sensation,* she thought. Christian and Janize showed up around ten o'clock. Introductions were made while Marcia sized up Janize and immediately signaled her approval.

"Now what?" asked Laurenz.

"Christian and Janize will go to the temple and stay close but apart," said Alaurenz. "The deviant Allfathers and the sub clergy scrutinize the young and single. We hope to put one or both of them in the inner sanctum of the temple where the Licentia does its dirty work."

"I will go too," said Marcia.

"Uh, I don't think that would be such a good idea," said Alaurenz.

"The Guardians, who are the secret police, are on the lookout for aberrant behavior. You could be detained. I was with Laurenz when we went the first time to tell him how to act. If you wish to go alone, you should be coached."

"Tell you what," said Laurenz casually. "Why don't you and Freda go out again and drink in the city, see the sights?"

Marcia eyed him sideways but saw Laurenz was depending on her to keep Freda occupied, so she would not cause trouble or get in the way.

"If you go near the temple, I would suggest that you view it from a distance and not try to enter," added Alaurenz.

"It can't be all that hard. Besides, what can they do to me?" said Marcia. "Tell me what to do?"

"The suppression broadcasts impede initiative, so if you get within several hundred yards, you have to mimic the behavior of those around you," Alaurenz explained.

Laurenz and Cralle worked furiously to clear the day's workload.

"There. That's the last of them," said Cralle. "If they used better components, they wouldn't fail so often. That one over there—shove it over. It was totaled by a falling tree. I think we can use the parts in a reactionary way by manipulating the circuitry. You break it down while I study this schematic."

They stared at the improvised gadget lying on the bench.

"How can we test it without giving ourselves away?" asked Laurenz.

"First of all, it is just a table strewn mess now, but I believe it will work," said Cralle. "We have to fix it together into a viable package as small as possible. Anything large would attract attention. It would be safest to test it in a typical area covered by the blanket broadcast, but the results would be subtle and difficult to observe. I would suggest during lunch hour we find a spot as secluded as possible just off the temple main way and target the worshipers as they enter where the Congregation cranks it up in order to have a docile and subservient audience."

Laurenz and Cralle strolled toward the temple with the nullifier now miniaturized and enclosed in an unobtrusive case. As they moved closer to the temple, Cralle said, "Veer left on the next crosswalk. It disappears into that coppice of trees and shrubs. Once out of sight, we can slip into the foliage, move to its closest abutment to the temple main way, and set up."

They peered through an opening in the bushes. The passage to the temple was now crowded with those drawn by the Breath of God broadcasts.

"Just a minute while I set up the power supply," said Cralle. "It's ready. We only need to test the momentary reaction of the masses to judge the effectiveness of it. We dare not linger too long."

"Okay, fire it up," said Laurenz, having by now eased comfortably into his role as a revolutionary.

Cralle activated the depressor and watched for some reaction in the crowd. At first, there was nothing. Then there was a subtle change. One, then another slowed and looked around. A Guardian shifted his bored stance to alertness as a pilgrim stopped and turned.

"Turn it off," snapped Cralle as Laurenz, who had observed the same deviant behavior, dived for the depressor. To the relief of both, the passage of the crowd resumed its normal flow, and the Guardians relaxed.

"It is going to work," said Laurenz. "But we need to decide whether to apply it here locally at the temple or try to ramp up its power and blanket the city."

"There is an argument for both," said Cralle. "We can take the chance of starting a revolution here at the temple and let the populace wreck the place and decimate the leadership, which may or may not be present. Or, we can hold it in reserve and follow the iffy path of trying for a complete nullification of the broadcast at the source with the hope it will spark a revolt in the general population."

"The problem with the second option is that in our world the populace is scattered—at work, in homes, in schools, and at a thousand other places," said Laurenz. "It would take time for the movement to gain momentum, also because it is an all or nothing course. The Congregation might be able to get its repressive act together enough to put down the uprising by reestablishing the broadcasts. The Guardians for sure would be out in force at the slightest hint of a breakdown."

"True, but the Guardians are vastly outnumbered should the people be aroused," said Cralle.

"It's a chance, but I think we should try to put the DDS transmitter out of commission and keep this portable suppressor in reserve to zap the temple should that fail," said Laurenz.

"Right. Now, for the transmitter, it will involve reaching the roof of the DDS and gaining access to the antenna," said Cralle. "For that, we will be operating blind, because the upper floors are off limits after the second level, which would suggest that the instruments generating the signal may be on the intervening floors."

"We shall have to wing it," said Laurenz finally. "Now, you are vulnerable. Why not let me go alone. If all fails, we can slip off to fight another day, and I can deactivate and just leave my shell."

"All right," said Cralle hesitantly. "Will you need explosives? If so, we will have to return to the facility and get them from Alaurenz."

"Right, so we will plan it for tomorrow," said Laurenz. "For now, we must get back to the DDS and finish the afternoon."

"By this time, the call to the midday services has been made," said Alaurenz, addressing Christian and Janize. "Those programed to attend are summoned. You must have guessed it since you drifted in on schedule before when the others were mustered."

"Yes, and I wanted to be someplace and got careless," said Janize.

"You know better now," said Alaurenz. "You will stay several paces ahead. When you reach the temple with no interference, Christian will sit just behind you. If you come and go free, we can try again at vespers or tomorrow."

Christian and Janize exited the lab and made for the temple, while Freda and Marcia wandered away.

"It's just like our world," said Freda as they strolled through the streets of Danvar.

"Not quite. Have you ever seen buildings that looked like that?" asked Marcia, indicating the surrounds.

"Well, maybe not," said Freda. "But the people seem to be going about doing the same things we do. There are shops, children at play, and others either at leisure or going about on some specific errand, business or personal."

"But have you noted the sedated look on their faces and the repressed character of their gate?" said Marcia.

"Yes, but I just assumed they have adopted that which we have always advocated—the universal use of the becalming substances, both as support for the travails of everyday life and as a path to the land of the spirit."

Marcia turned away momentarily to hide her reaction to Freda's musings. *How can one carry such a worldview when everything around her speaks of something different?*

They were crossing the main way leading to the temple, which stood not too distant towering above the landscape. A speckle of low-lying clouds swirled about its heights as a steady stream of pilgrims moved toward it.

Freda stopped. "What a wondrous sight. Surely the gods must congregate there. I must see it closer"

"Uh . . . well, I don't think that would be such a good idea," said Marcia. "Laurenz has warned us of certain . . . complications that can arise if the uninitiated venture too close," said Marcia.

"But what harm can come from it?" said Freda. "We are told that nothing can harm us in this spectral form."

Marcia surveyed the periphery of the main way for the dreaded Guardians Laurenz had spoken of. A sprinkling of black-clad dots could be discerned farther down nearer to the temple itself. "Maybe we can go just a little closer," she said cautiously.

They drifted along with the other pilgrims. The temple gradually loomed over them and cast an attenuated shadow with the sun eclipsed but not banished from the scene. Its corona burst from the flanks of the massive edifice giving the impression of godly power held in restraint.

"I must visit this place and tell our followers of its wonder and magic where at last, the issues of karma are resolved.

In this spiritual haven, we may well move beyond earthly limitations and reach nirvana," Freda droned.

"This is close enough," said Marcia with a sigh as she slowed and stopped. But under the spell of the temple, Freda kept walking.

"Freda!" Marcia force whispered as she scurried to keep up. "Laurenz warned us not to go too close. Freda!"

Freda moved forward in a trance. Marcia looked about. The flow had slowed slightly due to a change in the cadence of the crowd. An enforced regularity had seeped into the marchers. *We have entered the cranked up suppression field Laurenz talked about,* thought Marcia. *I've got to get Freda out of her trance. If she is retained, she might blab all over the place about the metaphysical, give away information about the insurgency, and get her polymeric fill fried in the—what was it?—the Cleansing Chamber.*

Marcia had just about caught up with Freda when she felt herself restrained from behind by a black-clad figure that had arrived unnoticed. *Damn. I was the one who broke the rhythm of the flow trying to catch up with that nut, Freda.*

She whirled and spoke harshly by instinct, instantly realizing her mistake.

"What on earth do you want? And take your hands off me."

The Guardian regarded her momentarily and hustled her forward toward the bowels of the temple. Marcia could still see Freda moving ahead with the other pilgrims some ten paces ahead. The herd entered the maw of the mammoth doorway and funneled into the seating area.

Freda melted into the temple and stood, mesmerized by the magnificent interior. The subtle variations from its counterpart back on Earth reinforced the fantasy that had overwhelmed her. She sank into a pew and soaked in the ritual. The short sermon was of the standard variety with customary universal admonishments to resist evil and devote service to the faith and Church. The service was drawing to a close when in smooth succession a group of worshipers similar to those around her were brought in. A chamber adjoining the altar was opened, and the docile subjects were herded inside. The grating noise and flash of light brought Freda to her senses. She gaped at the scene. The presiding priest opened the chamber to display the subjects who had willingly entered just a moment before. They were eerily still, like statues, as was the congregation. The service's closing episode was bizarre enough to jar her out of her dreamy trance. Her instincts took over.

That was strange. I wonder if something has happened to those people, and where is Marcia? She was with me till we entered.

Freda rose to leave and looked around. Still vaguely upset by the incongruous scene at the end of the service, she exited the temple. Her listless character and usual plodding gate helped her clear the closely monitored interval leading from the temple.

Now, where could she have gone? Oh my, if I can't find her, I will have to find my own way back to the laboratory. It must be in that direction.

XVII

All the earthlings assembled in Alaurenz' lab at the end of the day.

"Where are Marcia and Freda?" asked Laurenz. "They—"

The group was interrupted by a sound, an indication that someone had entered the outer confines of the lab.

"That must be them now," said Laurenz, gazing at the security monitor. "It's Freda. I wonder what happened to Marcia."

Freda entered through the locker door and strode toward the group, a slightly worried look on her face. "I lost track of Marcia and assumed that she would be here when I returned."

Laurenz was dumbfounded and a little annoyed but knew Marcia would simply disconnect and leave her shell if something unforeseen happened. "When was the last time you saw her?"

"It was when we were entering the temple. We—"

"You what?" sputtered Laurenz.

"You did what?" said Alaurenz, dovetailing Laurenz' outburst.

"I just had to see it. It was magnificent, perhaps the answer to our quest for the mecca of spiritual uplift. I look forward to our Coalition faithful members being able to visit it."

"Did—anything unusual happen?" asked Alaurenz tentatively.

"Well, yes, and puzzling. I'm only guessing, but they chose several of the worshipers for a special ritual. It appeared to be an infusion of some essence of godliness in a concentrated form, because they emerged from the process in a state of absolute calm."

Idiot. "Freda," said Laurenz barely under control. "That was an execution, the elimination of dissenters. They call it Cleansing. Do you understand me? They killed those people. I warned you before we left Earth that things here were not so rosy, and specifically not to go near the temple. Now just where is Marcia?"

"Well," whined an obviously shaken Freda. "She must have disappeared between the time we were just a few feet from the temple entrance to the end of the service, but during that time, I was lured into communion with the universal god on high and unaware of earthly happenings."

"Do you suppose she was taken by the Licentia?" said Alaurenz absently. "You would be a better judge than us about that," said Laurenz. "At least she is in no danger, but your plan is. If she has to abandon her shell in the bowels of the temple, it will raise suspicions that our penetration into the Congregation's affairs is more extensive than we would have them know. Marcia is in sympathy with your aims, however, and would only do that as a last resort. She will try to find some other way out. I may have to disengage and rouse Marcia to find out just where her hologram is, but first I will search for her myself and try to find her here"

"I will go too," said Cralle, impulsively and in a cloud of uncertainty.

"Okay," said Laurenz doing a double take.

Marcia, still restrained, was shunted to the side toward the door of a small holding chamber. They were about to enter when they were intercepted by a robed figure.

"Guardian, I will relieve you of this follower."

The Guardian shoved Marcia into the small room and moved just outside. Marcia could hear noises of heated conversation between him and the cleric, but she could not understand what they were saying. The Guardian, failing to convince the cleric that she was not under the control of the suppression signal, left in a huff. After a moment's pause, the cleric entered and declared, "You have been chosen for additional service to the Church."

"Christo," said Marcia under her breath, reverting to her native Portuguese. *This is what Alaurenz was talking about. I thought they only enlisted the younger ones. I have already goofed it. If they find out my true nature, all hell is going to break loose. I'll just play along. Maybe I can salvage something.*

The cleric led Marcia up a flight of stairs to a chamber where a woman stood waiting. The gnarled old hag attempted a limp smile but said nothing.

"Please prepare her for indoctrination," said the cleric.

I wonder what that means, thought Marcia.

The cleric left, and the old woman slunk over to one of the many cabinets that lined the room and laid out a neatly folded garment.

"Please put this on," said the woman in a husky voice.

Something about her gave Marcia pause. *The hands were besprinkled with hair, and on the face, there's the shadow of a beard. No doubt about it—this is a man, cross-dressed, someone they have put out of sight, an embarrassment even to the degenerate leadership.*

The "woman" stood quietly with a crooked grin on her face.

"I would like some privacy," said Marcia finally, hoping that with such a show of initiative she did not betray the absence of the controlling chip that was supposed to be implanted in her.

The woman bowed and left through a door not evident before. One of the many panels ringing the room had swung open, giving egress to the further recesses of the temple.

Marcia inspected the garment, which turned out to be a simple ankle-length sheath. *I need to get out of here now.* She inspected the door through which they had entered. A peek outside revealed nothing. *They must think that simple suggestion is enough to force compliance. Maybe if I put this thing on, it will attract less attention.* She donned the dress, which was roomy enough to cover her light undergarments, and again peeked out the door. Two prelates who were just passing turned, and she gave them a warm smile and disappeared back into the room. After waiting several moments, Marcia looked out again. One of the two she had seen before was there staring at her. *Uh oh—trouble.*

"I see you have accepted your calling to service," oozed the priest.

His robe suggests minor rank, thought Marcia. *It is of drab color and void of ornate accouterments, probably a middle-aged hanger-on, a little dim and unable to advance in the ranks of the Church.*

"In order to commune with the divine, you must give of yourself to those who represent it," he continued.

"I am ready to do so gladly," said Marcia, vying for time and at the same time looking for a way out.

A voice from behind broke the tension. "Deacon Rablace, are you not preparing the evening vespers? Your name appears clearly on the roster."

"Uh . . . er, yes Allfather Bakel. I was just going."

Rablace eyed Marcia and turned to go.

Bakel! That's the insurgency operative within the Congregation Alaurenz mentioned. Could there be more than one Bakel? Probably not of Allfather rank.

"Thank you for intervening," ventured Marcia.

Bakel paused and turned. It was an odd comment for one who was under the power of the suppression broadcasts. The two stood staring at one another, suspicious, neither wanting to commit to full revelation.

Finally, Bakel said, "May I examine you?"

Marcia made a quick decision. She backed into the room, followed by Bakel and closed the door. Pulling up the sleeve of her garment, she presented it to Bakel who ran his hand up the forearm to the biceps. The color was right, but when pressed, the skin and underlying flesh betrayed the true nature of her form, uniform elasticity with no bone structure.

"You are . . . not of flesh," he gasped. "What are you doing here? Are you allied with . . . with . . ." Still in fear of committing, he did not want to say it.

"Alaurenz, yes, and you are Allfather Bakel."

"Yes, how did you get here and why would—"

"It was an accident—a rather involved story that I don't have time to tell. Suffice it to say, I bumbled into this situation and am trying to extract myself without revealing anything about Alaurenz' plans. My name is Marcia. Can you ease me out of here without causing alarm?"

"I don't know. The cleric who captured you may object to the loss of a . . . a prime specimen, if you may accept my appraisal and take no offense. I outrank him, but he could cause enough fuss to cause an investigation. It is my understanding that if all else fails, you can just deactivate."

"True, but my remains will be here, and they alone will tell a story. They would be harder for you to dispose of than my functioning self, because I am mobile and the shell is not."

"Follow me, and we will see if I can run the gauntlet of the Licentia who has the run of this portion of the temple. I do not come here often as the activity repels me."

Allfather Bakel peered out the door—nobody in sight. "Come," he said softly.

"What about this white overdress I have on?" said Marcia. I still have my usual clothing on underneath.

"Better keep it on for now. It fits in with the setting. The flock is banned from this segment of the temple, so everyday clothes would signal that something was amiss. That will change if we can reach the public areas, so be ready to get rid of it."

They entered the hallway and started for the stairs—still nobody. As they started down the stairway, footsteps could be heard coming up toward them.

"If we meet anyone, let me do the talking," said Bakel. "Just look subdued and passive."

The square-based staircase descended with equal treads falling away at right angles, each segment terminating at regular intervals on a platform. As they bottomed out on one of the platforms, they met the on comer approaching from below.

The cleric appraised Bakel and his charge. "Allfather Bakel, I see you have finally joined us in the revelry that our privileged positions offer."

"Uh . . . yes, I have finally succumbed to it. The temptation was too great. Now if you will excuse me, there are things I must do," said Bakel with a wink.

Bakel and Marcia resumed their descent but felt the watchful eyes of the cleric on them as they came to the next level and disappeared out of sight.

"Hurry," said Bakel. "The bottom is near where we can escape into the core of the temple. There is a conspicuous door that we dare not use, because it is in plain sight. The route through the confessionals is a better choice. The priests use it to enter unseen into the procedure of confession. There you can jettison your white gown and slip out. I will get rid of it." He glanced at his watch. "A service is just concluding. Try to melt into the crowd and get out. The Licentia do not keep any records of who is recruited. They are barely tolerated by the hierarchy. Now, do you know the way back to the lab?"

"Yes, and thank you for everything," said Marcia.

"Good. Tell Alaurenz I will be in contact."

Marcia drifted with the pilgrims as they left the temple, being careful to do nothing that would draw attention to her. She passed back down the temple main way and through the wall of high trees, which cordoned off the park like an enclave, and several support structures of similar design, which contained the temple itself. Glancing back, she saw nothing suspicious—only the usual parade of slow-moving pilgrims with an occasional accent of black, the ever-present Guardians.

She considered. *Let's see, the lab should be in this direction.* The pedestrian traffic looked normal as she traversed the various neighborhoods dotting the city of Danvar. Finally the ramshackle facade of the quasi factory concealing the lab appeared just few blocks ahead. The passersby were fewer now with only an occasional worker-type in evidence. She was about to close in on the lab building when she felt a firm grip on her shoulder. She spun around and was confronted once again by the Guardian who had originally detained her.

"I spotted you as you left the temple area and followed you here," he snapped. "I gave you over to the priests. How did you escape, and what are you doing in this neighborhood? There is nothing here but cheap shops and small industry."

"I was released by the fathers as . . . an unsatisfactory candidate."

"That is not likely," said the Guardian in appraisal of his captive. "There is something going on here that needs to be investigated. You were obviously not under the magic spell of those who visit the temple. You will come with me to the Guardian headquarters for interrogation."

In the distance, Laurenz and Cralle had just emerged from the building housing the lab, and it took a few seconds for them to focus on the scene a block and a half away. Cralle elbowed Laurenz.

"I see. Keep walking," said Laurenz as they strolled toward the Guardian and his captive making small talk as they went.

They were some twenty feet away before Marcia, who was preoccupied with the Guardian, noticed them. Her change of focus made the Guardian turn.

He snapped, "They won't help you, so come along and cause no more trouble."

Cralle and Laurenz radiated superb apathy as they closed in on the pair and almost passed, but as they came abreast, Laurenz hurled himself on the Guardian who reeled backward as he became entwined in the doughy mesh of the polymeric appendages. The Guardian planted his legs apart to brace himself against the unstable whole whose center of gravity was pulling him backward and off balance. The target was too good to pass up. Cralle planted a kick into the man's groin, which nullified all resistance. Marcia was now free and stood apprehensively to the side.

"What should we do with him?" asked Laurenz as he regarded the doubled-up figure moaning on the walkway.

"We can't let him go. We may have to keep him captive till . . . uh, you know what," said Cralle, softly raising his eyebrows.

"Okay, I don't know how Alaurenz is going to take this," said Laurenz. "In any event, we have to get him trussed up, blindfolded, and secluded. The only place to do it is back at the lab."

With some difficulty, they uncurled the suffering Guardian and penguin walked him back to the building housing the lab. They waited for a reaction to their unscheduled return, which was long in coming. Alaurenz finally appeared and without saying anything hustled the group into the cavernous front quasi-factory along with their captive.

"What has happened?" he inquired with resignation.

"We know only this: The Guardian had detained Marcia for some reason, and we had to intervene," said Laurenz. "Marcia can fill us in on the rest, but first let's muzzle this guy and get him out of hearing." He motioned to a shelf nearby. "Cralle, throw that drop cloth over him and bind it at the neck. We can cut away the extra material later."

They secured the Guardian and moved out of earshot.

"Here's how it went," said Marcia. "I was pursuing an out-of-control Freda who was bent on entering the temple when I was detained by this Guardian and taken into the temple. A cleric stepped in and took charge of me for recruitment into the service of the Licentia. By some coincidence, the Allfather Bakel you had spoken of was in that corner of the temple on some errand. At first, he intervened not to free me but because the sub cleric had digressed from his assigned duties. Because the cleric had identified him by name, I took a chance that this was the Allfather Bakel you had spoken of. After a cautious exchange, I revealed myself as did he. He helped me escape. Unfortunately, I was spotted by the same Guardian as I was leaving the temple," continued Marcia. "He followed me here."

"Freda! This is all her fault," exploded a disgusted Laurenz. "When I get back, I'm going to send the whole UMC packing. Maybe it is ingratitude, but they have used us as much as we them. If they want to blab, we can deny or verify as suits us. Nobody can prove a thing about interworld travel. It's too far out. Our peers doubt on scientific grounds, and in the press, lacking evidence, only the tabloids would dare suggest we have done it."

"That's for you to decide back on your world," said Alaurenz. "For now, let's concentrate on fixing things here."

"We are set for tomorrow," said Laurenz. "We will forget the Licentia and concentrate on reaching the transmitting antenna with some explosives to total it. If we can prod the populace to some independent thinking, the Licentia thing will solve itself. Until then, all of us will return to Earth and attend to our needs there. For now we need a nook to discard our polymeric fills."

"Yes, any of the storerooms will be okay for that—out of the way and safe from some tech knocking you over," said Alaurenz. "Cralle and Janize can spend the night at the lab here or return home as they wish. We will dump the Guardian in one of our makeshift cells and memory erase him if necessary. We are not in the business of execution."

The Council convened in emergency session. Archfather Verkezian signaled for quiet. "I have called this meeting at the request of the Chief of the Guardians, but there is an additional unexplained happening to be discussed. The fathers of the Wing of Divine Pleasure have informed me of the unexplained disappearance of one of the subjects, a young woman."

"That bunch of perverts will do us in yet," interrupted Allfather Corvus. "We should have reined them in long ago. Why can't they look for pleasure within our circle like the rest of us do?"

"You may have a point, but perhaps we should look more closely at what has been reported. Allfather Bakel," said Verkezian, lifting his focus and voice to the rear of the assembly. "It is my understanding that you were the last one seen with this woman. Have you finally joined the Wing after your tenure of reclusive abstinence?"

"Quite the contrary," responded Bakel in calculated joviality over the wanton titters of the assembly. "I happened to be in the Wing on an errand and noticed that Cleric Ajurmand had in his charge a young woman, apparently a recent recruit, since she was clad in the Robes of Submission. I pointed out to him that he was on the roster for vespers and already late in fulfillment of his duties. I took charge of the young woman and placed her in one of the holding rooms. I have no idea what happened after that."

A moment of silence followed, leaving Bakel with the uneasy feeling that his explanation was only provisionally accepted.

"Be that it may, another development must come first. One of the Guardians is missing. Chief Ganderk will explain."

"He did not report in," said Ganderk. "As of now, he is incommunicado and possibly in the custody of the insurgency. Investigation shows that he never arrived home, which almost eliminates some personal indiscretion like drunkenness."

"I suggest we put all sectors on alert and step up the Cleansing of those whose deviation has been firmly established—and for safety, add those held and suspected," said Corvus. "We must eliminate this threat once and for all."

"That is a little extreme," said Verkezian. "We will keep the Cleansing only for those of proven opposition, since each episode brings relatives and associates out of the woodwork. Apparently the emotions of grief and anxiety overwhelm and nullify the effect of suppression signals. As to the Guardian, we should wait and see if his absence has a simple explanation. As for the woman, I suspect one of the clerics may have hidden her away."

The earthlings retired to the parking spot Alaurenz had provided and deactivated.

"I am famished," said Christian to the group as they emerged from their chambers.

"So am I," said Freda. "I know a health restaurant to supercharge us for tomorrow's adventure."

"Uh, Marcia and I already have plans," said Laurenz.

"I will join you, Freda," said Christian with a sly glance toward Laurenz.

"Okay, we will see you here tomorrow early," said Laurenz, whose fury had subsided. He was now in a state of wonder at Christian's sacrifice. *Either he's a team player or is vegetarian. In any case, it will get Freda out of our hair till tomorrow.*

All except Freda arrived on time the next day

"Where is she? We need to get this thing resolved so that we can concentrate on science for a change," said Laurenz as the group waited by transfer chambers. He turned to Christian. "How was it?"

"What?" asked Christian.

"The health food restaurant and . . . well, Freda."

"Not bad for both. Actually, she is more interesting than her prim, kooky manor would suggest. The United Mystics Coalition, in spite of its pie-in-the-sky outlook and dizzying array of rituals, has some very practical pursuits. They take their philosophy on diet to the schools and provide free items. They also have strong liaisons with segments of mainstream religions, for instance, the Jesuits, the Humanistic Jews, and the Buddhist Shaolin."

"The Shaolin? Isn't that a little on the rough side for a bouquet of flower children?"

Christian answered with a shrug as Freda swept in.

"I am so sorry I am late. While traveling through the grounds, there was a poor cat trapped in a tree, and I just had to lend assistance in its rescue."

Laurenz rolled his eyes and hustled them into their individual chambers.

"Nate, send me first. Then wait five minutes and send the others. If there are any surprises on Otherearth, I can deactivate and abort transfer of the others."

After the interval, Marcia, Christian, and Freda transferred safely to Otherearth and re inhabited their polymeric fills. Laurenz addressed the group.

"The rest of you stay here. Cralle will come with me for support in penetrating the upper floors of the DDS. He has more insight as to the layout of the headquarters building, because he is local. I will take the chances, and he will deny everything if caught. If I fail to destroy the transmitting antenna and nullify the Breath of God broadcasts, we will try something else."

"What should we do—that is, Freda and I?" asked Marcia, knowing that Laurenz had forgotten about the Freda problem.

"Uh—just cool your heels till we have it under control—or not. It is Alaurenz, Cralle, and Janize who risk most if we fail. The worst scenario is that we don't succeed, and the insurrection has to start again from scratch. We . . . what happened to Christian?"

"He's over there talking to Janize," said Marcia with a mixture of amusement and vague apprehension as a faint giggle emanated from the direction of the couple. "Apparently, they are hitting it off well."

Laurenz looked at the twosome and then at Marcia again.

"What?" asked Marcia, belatedly aware of Laurenz' pensive mood.

"Nothing." Something about those two gnawed at his senses, but the urgency of the moment kept clarity at bay.

Laurenz and Cralle were about to leave when Alaurenz said, "I will go the vicinity of the temple to monitor any change in behavior. If you are able to set off the charge, it should be heard all over, and I will use it as a cue."

Laurenz and Cralle approached the DDS building, flashed their IDs, and passed through security. Retiring to the lower level of their workstation, Cralle spoke.

"I have a plan that gives the best chance for you to reach the roof and the antenna," said Cralle. "We will launch the attack from here. You may have noticed the red door with the cross on it—not the inverted one indicating some religious connection, but the one having the well-known symbol indicating something prohibited. It obscures a feature typical of construction here. The door enters into the escape shaft for fire or other emergencies, which connects all floors with a spiral staircase. It is always locked and has an electronic key system that, when engaged, retracts both the dead bolt and spring latch. Its control is in the possession of a select few on each level. Once you enter, you can exit at any level. It will probably take you as far as the top floor. From there, you are on your own and will have to figure out how to get to the roof. Do you have the explosive pack?"

"I have it. Any suggestions as to what might be on that top floor?"

"Haven't a clue, but when you get there, do a careful look-see before stepping out."

"Can I get back into the shaft if I have to make a hasty exit, successful or not?" Laurenz asked.

"You may not have to. The explosion will cause chaos, and all levels will be evacuating by whatever avenues are available, including the emergency shaft. You may be able to melt into the stream and exit with the others. The disorder should prevent any careful scrutiny of the personnel."

"If you say so. Let's get on with it," said Laurenz. "So how do we get the door open in the first place?"

"All the lines run inside the wall to the side of the door," said Cralle. "I think I can do a surgical penetration of the area and short the controlling circuit. You keep watch while I work on the wall."

Cralle moved to the door and selected a spot down close to the floor least likely to be noticed. He chiseled out a small square revealing several color-coded wires. He considered for a moment and then cut two of them, stripping the insulation from the ends. He selected two of the leads and touched them together. A soft click emanated from the door.

"That did it," said Cralle. "You go ahead while I do a cosmetic patch on this hole here. Good luck."

Laurenz entered the shaft. It was just a Cralle had described. The spiral staircase was enclosed in a tight cylinder, and the view upward was blocked by the curl of the stairway itself. Laurenz sighed and plodded upward. At each level, the stair came to a square platform and a door. After ten flights or so, Laurenz came to a larger space. The crowded cylinder widened to several times its original diameter. A door was there and opposite, windows forming half a circle and giving view to the outside. In the near distance, spires of the temple loomed ominously. Laurenz tried the door, and as Cralle had said, it was unlocked. He eased it open a crack and peeked out. Some twenty feet away marked the edge of a labyrinthine cluster of office modules. The one whose opening faced him showed banks of computers and an array of multiple screens. Technicians who seemed to be dressed the same as he was randomly passed his field of view.

He considered. *This floor and perhaps some below monitor and control the behavior of the people through the embedded chips. I could slip in and blend in with the others, but if challenged, my ID might give me away. I must take that chance.*

He slipped out into the workspace and walked casually down the aisle flanked by stations manned by uniformed personnel eerily illuminated by blinking polka dots of light. Passing several cross isles which led to doors on his left, he chose one and approached it. *Locked—damn.* Laurenz tried two more isles and found the doors locked.

Slipping back to the door that led to the escape stairway, he paused—all quiet. He slipped back into the well of the spiral staircase and surveyed the enlarged, flattened cylindrical space that topped out the narrow tube containing the helical path upward that had brought him there.

The windows—I will check the view is outside.

Laurenz crossed over to the leftmost of the lot and peered out. The wall of the DDS building obstructed the view on the left, and craning his neck, he could just make out the edge of the roof.

Let's see if I can get this thing open. No, it's fixed. What the hell?

Laurenz aimed his dough-like elbow at the center of the glass. To his surprise, it shattered. The pieces flew into space and disappeared downward. He heard a faint crash and tinkle as they met the surface below. Peering out, he saw that although the escape shaft had been constructed within the confines of the building's structure, the enlarged cylinder atop was cantilevered out over the structure's walls covering the recessed area below.

Now, what I can to with this fake body of mine. It's certainly lighter than its equivalent in human flesh, and even though I cannot move fast, strength should not be an issue

Laurenz carefully removed the jagged edges of the remaining glass and placed them on the floor. *No sense in carving up a perfectly good polymeric fill,* he thought. He climbed out on the ledge and looked for something above to grasp onto—nothing. *No, wait,* he thought. He could just reach one of the ornaments that decorated the corners of the window opening. He grasped it and hoisted himself up. Grunt and muscle had no role. His hologram as pure energy had no weight in the earthly, non-Einsteinian realm. Only the foam-like polymer that filled it and the explosives packet vital to his mission were subject to gravity. But in Laurenz' form, the singular nature of the bond between the fill and hologram mandated that where one went, so did the other. *Where my holo goes, my fill goes,* he rhymed to himself.

Swinging his arm blindly in a vertical arc, he grasped the edge of the roof and pulled himself the rest of the way. Rolling over onto the flat surface of the roof, he found himself looking upward at the statue of the savior towering above. He righted himself and circled the enormous statue, which masked the BOG transmitting antenna.

There—that must be some sort of service door. He tried it. *Unlocked . . . a fortunate break.*

He moved inside. The graceful exterior of the statue covered an intricate cross trussing inside devised to support both the statue and the antenna it concealed. The tangle disappeared into the darkness above.

At the base, those leads feed the signal, thought Laurenz. *An explosion should sever them, trash the antenna support, and destroy a great part of the statue itself.*

Laurenz concentrated on placing the explosives for optimum damage and activating the timer Cralle had devised.

"Who is there?" said a voice from outside.

A uniformed silhouette appeared in the doorway, backlit by the morning sun.

"I said, who is there? This is a restricted area."

Laurenz emerged from behind the network of supports. "I came here for routine maintenance," said Laurenz with as much casualness as the situation would allow. He knew it would be unconvincing but was playing for time. He had just sixty seconds before the whole thing went up.

"Whoever you are, you are not authorized to be here. Come with me," he said, drawing some kind of weapon.

"I am sure I can provide an explanation to whoever may require it," said Laurenz.

The guard paid no attention to Laurenz as he hustled him to a doorway leading to the innards of the DDS. They were about to pass through when Laurenz bolted toward the point of the building where he had gained the roof. The surprised guard stood mesmerized by the sluggishness of Laurenz' movement, knowing he had essentially nowhere to go, and his rate of retreat was near comical.

His voice tinged with humor, the guard yelled, "Stop!"

Laurenz closed inexorably with the building's edge. The guard's view of a docile captive was shaken as Laurenz reached the roof boundary and launched into space. His awe was short-lived as a loud explosion sent pieces of the statue's base in every direction.

Laurenz' confidence in the imperviousness of his holographic form could not surmount the sense of vertigo he felt as he leapt into the void. The distinct emptiness that accompanies panic was there in stark reality. He was about halfway through his fall when he heard the explosion. As he twisted around to see the top of the statue move out of sight, he collided with the grassy surface of DDS building inset. He literally bounced pin wheeling uncontrollably until he settled in a corner of the lot.

That was scary, thought Laurenz as he righted himself and both felt and visually inspected his polymeric shell. *More or less intact . . . a little compression in my left shoulder where I first hit. I Must get to Cralle. My unexpected exit left him vulnerable inside the DDS.*

He circled the building to the front and met the pandemonium created by the explosion. The view upward presented a bizarre scene. Half of the torso of the savior statue hung precariously over the building's edge, with the face of the savior now facing downward.

He is looking at me—accusingly, thought Laurenz.

Some Guardians, staff, and a variety of the unidentified were running toward the center of the chaos, but most were running away. Laurenz was about to squeeze passed the outflow when he met Cralle. Cralle had a sardonic expression on his face, which morphed into relief, as he identified his coconspirator. The two said nothing as Laurenz reversed direction and joined Cralle to distance them from the havoc, which still engulfed the DDS.

"Let's see how the populace is reacting to the absence of BOG broadcasts," said Cralle when they were safely away.

They strolled through the streets of Danvar and began to notice several people stop and look around confused.

"Over near the temple should give us an even better test of the effect," said Laurenz

Closer to the temple it was obvious that something had happened to change things. Instead of a steady flow of worshipers, many were engaged in animated discussion. Closer in, where the suppression was routinely enhanced, there was a cluster of Guardians and more pilgrims.

"Let's check that out," said Cralle. "It looks like the Guardians may have met their match."

"Yes, but not too close," said Laurenz. "We don't want to get caught up in a sweep. The numbers seem to be evenly matched."

"At that exact spot, yes, but look at those on the periphery," said Cralle. "Many are watching from a distance. Any punitive action by the Guardians could trigger a response, and they know it. After all, the people are aware they are manipulated but have been powerless to do anything about it, because of the suppression and the knowledge they would increase it at any hint of a disturbance. They can't do that now."

They stood watching for a few more minutes. Flow into the temple had all but stopped, and several who had entered were leaving. A few Allfathers could be seen in the entranceway.

"Let's return to the lab and wait to see if the people are liberated enough to take care of things themselves," said Laurenz.

XVIII

A pounding on the door of Archfather Verkezian's chamber jarred him from his customary midday slumber. Plodding to the door, he opened it to an anxious Allfather Leeche.

"Archfather, there has been an explosion at the Diocese of Devine Science building, and the becalming broadcasts have been disrupted."

"How could that have happened?" said Verkezian, instantly alive.

"They sabotaged the transmission point—the antenna on the roof of the building."

"Did anybody see who did it? And how was he able to reach the roof without being detected?"

"We have a report from one of the guards that he engaged the culprit at the base of the broadcast tower. He said that the culprit had on the uniform of a DDS technician. The guard is going through personnel photos to identify him. He was a fanatic of some sort, because he leapt from the roof in a suicide bid just before the explosion. No body has been found, so we have surmised that his coconspirators removed it before we could retrieve and identify it."

"What is the reaction of the populace? Are they agitated or aware of what is going on?"

"There are signs of it, especially near the temple where the suppression is greatest. The programed quota of worshipers never appeared or refused to enter the temple as they neared. As a consequence, the morning service is playing to an empty audience as we speak. The Guardians and security are assessing the dam—"

"What happened?" cut in Allfather Corvus, newly arrived. "I heard the explosion from the direction of the DDS headquarters, looked out, and saw that the statue with the savior had fallen and I assume with it, the broadcast antenna. Does this mean that the suppression broadcasts are down?"

"Here locally and in the provinces fed from here," said Archfather Verkezian. "But we hope to have it up and running as quickly as possible, and it has compromised the control of the rest of the country. The feed from the transmitters to the provinces is down for now."

"The central authority lies here in the leadership and the power of the temple as projected through the Holy Television Network," said Corvus. "The Cleansings we show cut through the fog of the suppression, strike subliminal fear in the flock, and promote public order, but a disruption here could metastasize quickly and lead to a general uprising."

"I will call an emergency meeting of the Council now," said Verkezian.

The Council of the Devine Congregation of Infinite Wisdom met in a frantic session. The Council room was alive with the rustle of clerical garments, the tinkle of their accouterments, and hushed exchanges of the Allfathers.

"Is Romarda here yet?" inquired Verkezian through the din.

"I have not seen—"

"Here," said Romarda, cutting of Corvus. Romarda had just arrived along with Chief Ganderk.

"Adjunct Father Romarda, how quickly can the broadcasts be up and running?" asked Verkezian.

"The technicians are working on it now," said Jurse Romarda. "The backup system will be at reduced intensity and sufficient strength to keep down any revolt but not enough to induce the periodic summons to the temple."

"Chief Ganderk, put the Guardians on increased alert but direct them to avoid incidents. And suspend the services till we can restore the full suppression," ordered Verkezian. "If we can contain things here in Danvar, the provinces will make no trouble."

The council dissolved amid feverish discussions among the Allfathers. Verkezian took Romarda aside. "How did he get on the staff in the first place?" asked Archfather Verkezian.

"We traced the records after the technician identified him. He was recommended by Allfather Bakel, along with another who had been through our Technical College," said Romarda. "The two were working as a team in maintenance."

"Bakel again," said Verkezian. "This has gone beyond coincidence. He must answer for this. As for the two he recommended, they were both probably in on it. Since the one who leaped is probably dead, let's see how his colleague and, for that matter, Father Bakel himself reacts to the news. Fetch him here. Tomorrow we will see if the surviving one shows up for work."

Alaurenz greeted Cralle and Laurenz with relief as they arrived at the lab where Alaurenz, Janize, and the other holo-formed earthlings waited. "When we heard the explosion in the distance and the Holy Television Network went to unscheduled programming, we knew that you had at least some success. What did you observe in the populace?"

"Are you all right?" asked Marcia, cutting in. Even though she was aware that Laurenz could not be harmed, she had herself succumbed to the reality of the otherworld experience.

"Okay, just fine," assured Laurenz, first addressing Marcia. "Not too much," he said addressing to Alaurenz. "We took a sample of what effect it is having and found mixed results. We will have to wait and see if the suppression broadcasts will be down long enough to churn a general rebellion. That would most likely show itself in a march on the temple."

Hours passed, and signs that a general uprising had taken place failed to come. At about four o'clock in the afternoon, the Holy Television Network broadcasts resumed their normal schedule with special news bulletins explaining the disruption in the public tranquility and warning the culprits of reprisals to come.

"The BOG transmissions must be back up," said Alaurenz. "It looks like we failed."

"Back to the drawing board," said Laurenz. "Alaurenz, is there some way we can smuggle the portable suppressor into the temple and target the pilgrims in the act of worship? If we can get them released just before a Cleansing ritual, it could elevate fury to a point that it cannot be contained."

"I will have to consult Allfather Bakel about that. He might have an angle," said Alaurenz. "Another question is should Cralle and I return to work at the DDS as usual and take a chance that they will not connect us with the incident, or should we fade away? In that case, Cralle, at least, will be a fugitive."

"That leaves us with a dilemma," said Alaurenz. "They may have already identified you from interrogating the guard who encountered you on the DDS roof. Even worse, it may implicate Allfather Bakel who recommended you for the jobs. He will have a hard time explaining it away."

"If we don't show up, it will definitely implicate Bakel," said Laurenz. "If we do, maybe we can fake our way through, insist we were on the job at the time, and suggest that the tech on the roof made a mistake. After all, I am supposed to be dead. No normal person could survive that fall from the roof of the DDS."

"It's worth a try, but at the first sign that it isn't flying, bolt," said Alaurenz. "Hopefully we can warn Bakel in time for him to go underground."

"For now, I think our Earth group should go dormant till tomorrow and tend to our bodily needs," said Laurenz. "We are all tired from being sequestered and need some food, exercise, and mental rest from the tension here. In the meantime, see what develops and plan for Cralle and me to show up for work as usual at the DDS."

Alaurenz was stuck with a pile of uncertainties but was also acutely aware of the stresses of interworld travel. He nodded his assent. As the four earthlings retired to a corner and again deactivated, the silent exchange passing between Christian and Janize did not escape the notice of Laurenz or Marcia.

Allfather Bakel received the summons with alarm but went immediately to the Archfather's chambers where Verkezian waited along with Romarda.

"You summoned me, Archfather? What sort of service can I provide the Congregation?"

"Perhaps you can explain to us about the two technicians you recommended to the DDS. We have located one of them in the records of registration along with his suppression codes," said Verkezian as Romarda stood in silence. "His name is Cralle Damon. There is nothing overtly suspicious about him. The other person, a Laurenz Kaplow, is unfortunately listed as disappeared. They—well, one of them at least—have been involved in the recent attempt to disrupt the BOG broadcasts."

"This is shocking!" said Bakel, feigning outrage. "Are you sure of this? The men were recommended to me by my secular acquaintances for their expertise and sincere allegiance to the principles of the Congregation. How could they have been so corrupted?" Playing for time, Bakel persisted. "Couldn't you even now activate their dormant controlling chips? After all, we all are endowed with a code at birth that permits selective manipulation of problem citizens."

"We are searching the registry at this moment to do just that," said Verkezian. "For now, the finger of suspicion points to your friends and, unfortunately, to you yourself who recommended them. I will suggest that you remain confined to your chambers until this can be resolved. On top of this, I was not entirely satisfied at your explanation of the disappearance of the woman from the Wing of Devine Pleasure."

"I will gladly do as you wish, but I hope you do not suspect me of involvement in this outrage against the Congregation," said Bakel as he turned to go.

After Bakel left, Verkezian spoke to Romarda.

"Why didn't we catch this when these men were processed?" asked Verkezian

"There was no reason to cross-check," said Romarda. "A live person shows up, and we assume he is a person of record."

"That is something we will have to correct if the insurgents are an assembly of the so-called missing," said Verkezian.

XIX

The earthlings emerged from their chambers blinking, each stretching in a corporal counterpoint.

Freda was the first to speak. "I hope we can get out a little more tomorrow to explore the marvelous world you have discovered. Surely any dispute with the Church, the Congregation as you call it, can be resolved amicably to the satisfaction of all. I am still little disturbed at the ritual I witnessed, which you have described in the most abject terms, but I am sure it has an innocent explanation. Also, I was strolling through a park when I heard that explosion. I hope no one was hurt."

"All of us need some rest and to be fresh for the return to Otherearth tomorrow," said Laurenz, breaking the silence following Freda's naive comment. "We need to get this thing resolved as soon as possible, as we all have other priorities. I am sure you all look on this as some sort of bizarre adventure, but the breakthrough we have made in interworld contact is far more important than the irritating internecine bickering on Otherearth. Be back here at 7:00 a.m. tomorrow to transfer. Cralle and I are going to show up for work and see what happens."

Freda and Christian started to leave when Laurenz said, "Christian, stick around for a moment. Uh, maybe you would like to get a bite with Marcia and me?"

"Okay," said Christian. Turning to Freda, he said, "Freda, I'll see you tomorrow."

Marcia, sensing what Laurenz was up to, said nothing. They made their way to a local restaurant and settled down.

Laurenz hesitated then spoke easily. "You and Freda seem to have made friends. I appreciate your and Marcia's efforts to keep her out of our hair. Oh, and I see that you and Janize have uh . . . bonded, for want of a better word, quite thoroughly."

"Oh yes, she's quite a girl—smart, cute," said Christian enthusiastically. "I think she likes me too. She wants to get together after we resolve this thing and show me the live spots of Danvar, which promise to be even more lively when and if the suppression is lifted. She—"

"Christian," Laurenz broke in seriously. "I have seen the way she looks at you. I must remind you that she is a real person, a flesh-and-blood female."

Christian's face was a mask of confusion. Marcia stared off into space.

"How would you expect to . . . to, that is, to respond with affection should things escalate?" said Laurenz.

"Well I . . . I—"

"He's right," said Marcia, whose eyes now focused on a befuddled Christian. "I have a feeling she hasn't really thought it through herself. It would be the same only reversed if she came here."

"So what should I do?" mumbled Christian. "I thought about her all through our last come-back period and couldn't wait till we returned this morning."

"For now, just cool it," said Laurenz after a moment. "Maybe we can figure something out." *As of now, neither of us would have the foggiest of what that might be.*

They all gathered to transfer the next day. Freda, for a change, was on time and had a new look. A pantsuit of sorts had replaced the long floral dress, and the excessive accouterments that had always identified her were reduced to a single strand of jade beads. Her hair fell neatly as before, half eclipsing her pasty, minimally made-up face.

"Freda! You look downright stylish," said Laurenz as he and the others gaped.

"I thought of it as generic and more appropriate for the other-world. I take it we do not want to attract undue attention until we reveal ourselves as ambassadors of good will to our other-fellows who journey with us to paradise."

The things she can come up with. "Oookay," said Laurenz hesitantly while brows knit as the others tried to parse what Freda had just said.

On Otherearth, Alaurenz met the group with heightened anxiety. "Bakel is incommunicado. The usual channels of communication with him are cut off. I fear he is at least under suspicion and may have been detained."

"What do you suggest?" asked Laurenz. "Can we penetrate the innards of the cathedral where I assume the Allfathers reside?"

"Maybe, but for now we need to take one thing at a time," said Alaurenz. "We must find a more permanent way to blank the suppression broadcasts. You and Cralle report for work as planned and let them react. If it gets hairy, Cralle, protect yourself with that weapon you carry, and you and Laurenz get out of there. The rest of you do not wander too far till we see how this shakes down. First, we must again impart the essential solidity to your forms and then get to it."

Cralle and Laurenz entered the DDS building and were immediately taken several floors below to a holding room to await interrogation. None other than Chief Ganderk himself appeared almost immediately, momentarily at a loss for words by the appearance of Laurenz, who was supposed to be dead from the leap from the DDS building.

"You have been identified by a witness as the instigator of the sabotage to the . . . uh, statue of the savior," said Ganderk, uncertain of revealing what the statue itself concealed to anyone of minimum clearance.

"Sir, we were at work on the second under level when the outrageous event occurred," said Cralle. "The witness you refer to must be mistaken. We all look alike in this uniform. We evacuated with the others when it happened and have now returned to do our part in service to the Congregation."

Ganderk was a bundle of indecision. "There is too much to be explained here. I will retain you until you can be identified by the guard who was witness to your crime. And you," he added, addressing Laurenz, "you may also be able to explain why you are listed as missing in the records."

They were taken down several levels to a holding room. After an extended wait, Ganderk reappeared along with the guard who encountered Laurenz on the roof of the DDS building.

"That's him! Or at least it looks like him," said the guard. Turning to Laurenz, he added, "But surely you could not have survived the leap from the top of the building."

"Sir," said Laurenz, again addressing Ganderk. "I have no idea what he is talking about. My colleague and I were just as shocked by the explosion as you. As for my status as missing in the records, I was unaware of it. It is undoubtedly some clerical error, because I am standing here."

The guard stood looking at Laurenz uncertainly and then said, "But he even sounds like the man I met on the roof."

"That's enough for me," said Ganderk with tenuous resolve. "You will be held here until we can interrogate the both of you. You will not be able to keep secrets for long after my men get hold of you. And if guilty, your fates will serve as a potent demonstration to those who might oppose the Guardians and the Congregation."

Cralle tensed and started forward in a move toward the two, but Laurenz restrained him by grabbing a handful of shirt at his back. The gesture rocked Laurenz forward as Cralle's superior weight asserted itself on his flimsy polymeric fill. Laurenz was quick to cover the action by moving a few steps toward Ganderk and saying, "We will gladly await the opportunity to clear ourselves of these unfortunate charges and will hold no grudge when we are exonerated."

With a grunt, Ganderk exited. They heard the click of the door lock, signaling that the room was sealed from the outside. Laurenz was quick to explain to the hyper Cralle.

"I figured we would have a better chance of getting out of here by stealth rather than running the gauntlet of unknown stairways and guards. Maybe this was not such a good idea after all. We should have cut our losses and gone underground."

"It was mostly for Bakel," said Cralle. "A mole on the inside is invaluable to let us know just what the Congregation is doing, but what do we do now?"

"This room was not designed for detention. It is the location of opportunity, handy for whatever plans they have for us. Maybe that door can be breached in some way," said Laurenz as they both moved closer. "The pins on those hinges are on this side, but we don't have anything to pry them out. They are probably rusted too. Let's check out those cabinets over there."

Cralle rummaged through the shelves. "It's mostly soft stuff for cleaning. No, wait . . . This may be some kind of lubricant. And what's this?" Some tools.

"Bring the lube here and the tools. We can try to soften up the pins and housings," Laurenz suggested. He examined the container and gave a sniff. "It's oil-based all right. I'll douse the hinges."

He examined the tools which suggested the bare minimum needed for routine jobs. "I'll start on the bottom hinge with this hammer and screwdriver." Laurenz inserted the screwdriver in the furrow between the pinhead and joint housing and after several taps widened the gap.

"Hand me that lube," Laurenz said.

After another dousing and a few more taps, the pin broke free as the lube began to do its work. He worked on the second hinge, and it responded more easily, as did the remaining top one. They stood gazing at the door, which remained fixed in position by friction.

"I will pry the door out on the hinge side with this hammer," said Laurenz. "You stand here to catch it when it slips free on the dead bolt side. If it falls freely, it will wake the dead."

With a scraping sound, the door lurched and came free on the hinge side. Cralle caught it and lowered it slowly to the floor. Without hesitation, they moved into the hallway. They approached the lift and saw that its down signal was lit.

"That may be Ganderk and his goons," said Cralle. "We have to get away from here. I noticed that the lift that brought us here went no farther down, but I know there are floors below, which means they have a separate access. There's something special down there."

"That stairwell," Cralle said pointing. "Let's try that. They will come running when they discover we are gone. Wait! I want to take that hammer in case I have to crush some kneecaps."

Cralle returned, retrieved the hammer, and stuck it in his belt. He and Laurenz then rushed to the door leading to the stairwell, entering just as the down light on the lift went out. Bounding up several flights of stairs, they stopped when the symbols indicated ground level. Laurenz tried the door.

"Locked, damn."

"This is a general-use stair at ground level, so security probably keeps it sealed," said Cralle. "Besides, I'm sure Ganderk has alerted security on this floor by now. We should go down, even with all the unknowns."

"You're right," said Laurenz. "And if we go up farther, we're likely to meet that army of personnel I encountered on my sortie to destroy the antenna."

They started back down.

"Let's hope we don't meet Ganderk coming up," said Cralle.

But just as they reached one of the landings, they heard the sound of footsteps coming up from below.

"Ganderk is taking no chances," said Laurenz. "We have to make the most of it. Cralle, get that weapon of yours ready."

The footsteps came closer and as Cralle and Laurenz turned a corner, they met two Guardians moving up toward them.

"Stop," said one as Cralle and Laurenz continued downward.

"Let us pass. We are late and have to get back to our—"

That was all that Cralle got out before Laurenz launched himself down, closing on the two with arms and legs extended like a giant gingerbread cookie. His weight of forty pounds or so, consisting solely of the polymeric fill, enveloped the Guardians in the spongy mess that made up his Otherearth presence and gave Cralle enough time to reach the scene and use his stunner.

"How long will they be out?" asked Laurenz.

"Fifteen, maybe twenty minutes," said Cralle. "Long enough for us to get below, but we—or should I say I—will be trapped down there unless we can think of something. That's the nerve center of the DDS, the conduit for the subterranean power lines coming in and radiating to the outside. It's also the location of the backup should it be down."

"Maybe we can compromise it," said Laurenz as they continued downward.

The stairs finally terminated in a larger space. Several doors leading to places unknown ringed the enclosure with small wire-meshed glass windows affording view of the interior. The distinct hum of large machinery emanated from beyond the doors. They tried the doors—locked, as expected.

"Stand back," said Cralle as he swung his hammer at the glass, which splintered but remained in formless mass. A few more swings, and the opening was cleared.

"I'll see if I can reach the latch inside," said Cralle.

"Let me. My arms are longer, and I am in no danger of rasping myself on those sharp edges," said Laurenz, pointing to a fringe of irregular glass that remained on the periphery of the window.

After several grunts and much swearing, Laurenz reached the latch, and the door clicked open. They entered and surveyed the interior, a vast floor area covered with a neat array of generators that stood idle.

"This is much larger than the footprint of the building above. It must extend far under the adjacent buildings and yards," said Laurenz.

Cralle panned the wide expanse. To their left stretched out in a row were numerous doors leading to the unknown. About halfway down the length was a break. Just visible was a series of tanks.

"Those are the fuel tanks for the backup generators," said Cralle. "See if you can drain those tanks to disable the backup, while I try to cut the incoming power lines. If we succeed, we can blackout the whole complex and stop the BOG transmissions and possibly the Holly Television Network extending to the provinces. Our pursuers will be working blind."

"Right, but we will be running blind too," said Laurenz. "First we need to find some kind of emergency light ourselves. You trace the lines while I see if I can drain the tanks and rummage those rooms over there for a light. We must hurry. It is just a matter of time before they figure out that we are down here."

The pair separated. Laurenz found the critical valves, and a black, gooey substance began to cover the floor. Minutes passed before Laurenz emerged from one of the various chambers abutting the maze of machinery.

"I think I have—" said Laurenz, looking around for Cralle who was nowhere to be seen. "Cralle!"

"Down here," said Cralle, his voice echoing from a remote recess of the enclosure.

Laurenz followed the sound and eventually spotted Cralle kneeling next to the wall.

"I am sure this is it," said Cralle. "Look at the size of that conduit. There is enough juice coming through there to light a small city."

"How do you cut something that big without electrocuting yourself? What can we do to it?" said Laurenz.

Cralle considered. "Nothing mechanical like a saw for sure. The minute it shorted, sparks would fly all over the place."

"Yeah, a real Fourth of July," Laurenz agreed, "and you shouldn't be too close to the celebration."

"A what?"

"Never mind," said Laurenz, once again forgetting he was in a place with a different history.

"Did you see any welding equipment when you were rummaging around?" asked Cralle.

"Yes, as a matter of fact, there was a room full of the stuff where I found these lanterns."

"Can you find it again and roll a tank and torch down here?"

"I think so," said Laurenz as he wandered off, retracing his path.

A few minutes later, the creak of a hand truck signaled Laurenz' return. "Did you do the fuel tanks?" asked Cralle.

"Yes, and there's a slimy mess down there."

Cralle readied the torch and assessed the situation. "Stand back . . . and get that lantern ready."

Cralle methodically carved away the conduit, exposing the lines. "Now, here goes the first of the lot. I'll try to sever one lead at a time. If any of the hot stuff melts and flows over to the other lead, it will short, and maybe a breaker will trip. Either way, we may have to finish the job in the—"

They were interrupted by voices echoing through the cavernous expanse.

Cralle set to work, and after what seemed like an endless period, the space went dark.

"Christ—black as coal," said Laurenz as he fumbled with the lantern.

"Shine it over here," said Cralle as he concentrated on the feed lines.

"Wrap it up," said Laurenz. "This light makes us a target. We need to go dark to be on even terms with our pursuers."

"Just a sec," said Cralle as he cut the other lead. "That's it. They won't get that up and running anytime soon. Douse that light."

The darkness closed over them.

"Wait a little. Maybe we will adapt to it," said Laurenz uncertainly.

"Don't bet on it," said Cralle. "There is absolutely no light leaking from anywhere. But if they get something lit, the wash may at least give us some shadows to maneuver around and, even better, will tell us where they are."

"I got an idea of the general layout here," said Laurenz. "The machines are arranged in a grid, so I think we can feel our way back down the most remote corridor to the exit by bearing left to the wall and then right. By now, the place is probably in chaos again, and we may be able to melt into the crowd to get out."

They felt their way to their left, which led to the path between the machinery farthest from the path that had taken them there. A loud whine and grinding sound broke the silence, and the lights flickered on. The backup generators had engaged.

"Down!" said Laurenz. "They must have—"

As they crouched behind one of the machines, the lights flickered and darkness descended once again.

Cralle chuckled. "The generators had only the fuel residue in the pipes. The backups should now be out for good. I got a glimpse of the path forward, though. We are clear down to the far wall containing the entrance."

They moved cautiously through the darkness. All of sudden, there was a burst of unfamiliar language to their far right, interrupted by Cralle's snickers.

"I don't know what he said," said Laurenz. "But the tone was unmistakable. Was that Otherearth's rendition of profanity?"

"Excellent example," said Cralle with a stifled snicker. "They must have blundered into the thick goo of the fuel spill."

Another minute later, Cralle said, "We must be near the—"

The vague ambience of distant light suddenly cast dim shadows on the walls of the enclosure.

"They have some lanterns like ours," said Laurenz. "At least we will know where they are. Quick—we are almost to the exit."

The two rushed to the door leading back to the stairwell. A shout from the rear signaled that they had been discovered. Laurenz snapped on the lantern, and the two bounded up the stairs. As they approached ground level, they began to meet others who were groping their way upward and out and who welcomed the feeble light Laurenz was carrying.

"I wonder what happened to those two guards I zapped," said Cralle. "We sure haven't come across them."

"The group who flushed us in the machine room probably cleared them out," said Laurenz. "Ganderk probably removed them in order to not panic the DDS staff."

There was a crush at the ground level, and security was in confusion as a herd of employees streamed out.

"Separate but keep in sight," said Cralle as they joined the flow.

At last, they were free of the building. Laurenz joined Cralle, and they left the area.

"Well," said Laurenz with a sigh. "We certainly didn't plan the day like this, but it has turned out well. We have totaled the local suppression and shut down the Holy Television Network. Now let's see what the populace does. They got a taste of freedom the first time. This time, it will take forever to get the BOG back on line."

XX

Chief Ganderk spoke gravely into the phone. "The power is down in the DDS building, and the techies are unable to transmit the submission signal. It is again the work of that pair of techies who were implicated in the first attack. They had the audacity to show up for work this morning. They escaped our hold and managed to ravage the power source. They are still at large, but that colleague of yours who recommended them must be forced to reveal what he knows. I am declaring martial law here in Danvar and in the provinces,"

"What?" questioned Archfather Verkezian. "The situation is critical, but you cannot do that without my permission."

"Accept reality," snapped Ganderk. "Your supposed authority exists only with the cooperation and enforcement power of the Guardians. Even the DDS is subservient to us. You will close the temple to worshipers till further notice. Your silly rituals with the obligatory summons and executions have lost their value and have always had the potential to inflame the populace."

"This is a military coup d'état plain and simple. I will—"

The line went dead.

Verkezian called an emergency meeting of the Congregation.

"You have heard about the outage at the DDS. It was caused by the same elements that destroyed the statue of the savior and put the BOG suppression down before. Now with the latest sabotage, we are unable to broadcast either the BOG or the Holy Television Network, although our local outlets are continuing to press our message. Allfather Bakel knows something, and we must get it out of him. In addition, we have another problem on our hands. Ganderk has declared martial law and has threatened to take over the government. When I talked to him, he made disparaging remarks about the Congregation and trivialized our mission."

"He's trying to save his own neck, but he may be partly right," said Allfather Corvus. "He knows if we go down, he will too. The thing we need to do is keep him subservient to us without alienating the ranks of the Guardians. I suggest we enlist our Holy Guard of the Congregation to kidnap and quietly cleanse him. As far as Bakel is concerned, maybe we should cleanse him too."

Archfather Verkezian was taken aback and struggled for words. Allfather Flecthrum spoke after a pause. "Such extreme action would set our already tenuous hold on power teetering on the brink."

Another period of silence passed. Allfather Leeche finally spoke cautiously. "Do you think we could get to Ganderk? He rarely comes to the temple except for meetings like this, and I assume he was not invited to this one. Besides, if we rely on Jarbroak, who is next in command, to stay loyal, we may be making a mistake. He may be more radical than Ganderk."

"I know Jarbroak. He is piece of fluff, a fat hanger-on," said Allfather Corvus sharply. "Ganderk only keeps him there because he doesn't interfere."

"I will call another meeting and invite him to present his case," said Verkezian, apparently convinced by Allfather Corvus's drastic suggestion. "We can have the Holy Guard secure and seclude him. In the meantime, lock down Allfather Bakel. He may be innocent, but we cannot take the chance. We must cleanse him to prevent further erosion of our authority."

Laurenz and Cralle were greeted by the others as they made it back to the lab.

"What went on over there?" said Alaurenz. "The Holy Broadcast Network is down again."

"Not only that, but the submission transmission is down too," said Laurenz.

"That explains it," said Alaurenz. "I have seen small groups of citizens beginning to assemble throughout the city."

"Yes, hopefully these will coalesce into larger groups and generate leaders," said Cralle.

"The idea to go back to the facility this morning like nothing had happened didn't work, but it turned out well," said Laurenz. "They called our bluff and tried to detain us, but we managed to escape to the innards of the facility and blank the power supply. They will not have it up for some time. We don't know what effect it is having on the temple, but for certain, the pervasive summons to the temple is missing."

"As the populace becomes aware, they will be churning with resentment," added Cralle.

"Good. We will see just how far it goes, but from what you have told me, I fear for Bakel's safety," said Alaurenz. "He has surely been implicated as one of the perpetrators of the mischief you have mentioned."

"It's been boring around here—not even a deck of cards," said Marcia. "Maybe some of us holos could go over to the temple and extricate Bakel."

"Not a good idea," said Laurenz, succumbing to ill-defined fears. "Besides, even though it is just midday, I am bushed. Cralle and I went through a complex and rather stressful set of actions this morning. I need to get out of my Earth chamber for some exercise and real rest."

"Alright," said Alaurenz after a pause. "But we must keep the momentum of the insurgency. If the people are marching on the temple and fermenting general unrest, we should join in. And there is still the problem of Bakel. We cannot delay too long our efforts to rescue him."

We at least need to do that, thought Laurenz. *Beyond that, it is Alaurenz's fight and an issue for Otherearth. Maybe we have gotten too involved. After all, the scientific breakthrough of interworld travel is an advance for both of us. He has a stake in it too.*

"Let me recoup, and we will deal with it tomorrow," said Laurenz. "Come on, gang, let us retire to our parking spaces and deactivate. Christian, we are leaving."

The young Brazilian was in a corner engaged in a giggle-fest with Janize. Giving her a peck on the cheek, Christian joined the others for deactivation.

A circumspect Laurenz turned away musing. *That kiss . . . must have purely psychological rewards. He couldn't have actually felt anything. What the hell. Maybe that's enough.*

Jurse Romarda approached the Holy Guard standing outside Allfather Bakel's door. Although the scientific community had its own living space adjunct to the DDS, he had clearance to be there.

"I need to consult with Allfather Bakel," said Romarda.

"I am told he is to be detained," said the confused guard, "but . . . it was not specifically ordered that he was not to have visitors."

"It is precisely related to the reasons for his detention that I am here," said Romarda, firmly harnessing a piece of the truth to fit his ends.

The guard hesitated and then opened the door to Bakel's chambers.

Bakel, pouring over one of his many books, looked up. "Mr. Romarda," said Bakel, recognizing the scientist and waxing faux enthusiasm, "What a pleasant surprise."

Romarda was silent for an extended period as Bakel sat uncomfortably. "You have been connected to the insurgency," he said finally.

"It is a series of unfortunate coincidences. The men I recommended to the DDS were acquaintances of friends. I made the unfortunate decision to present them when I knew so little of their background."

"And what of the recruit's disappearance from the Licentia chambers?"

"That too has been explained. After I took charge of her from one whose ritual obligations had been neglected, she disappeared on her own."

"We have only your word for these 'coincidences.'"

Another lapse followed as Romarda rose and stared out the window. "The Congregation has overreached," he said without turning. "I know there are some among the Allfathers who share this view."

Is this some kind of opening? Even though an understatement, it is certainly the kind of thing he would not say openly, thought Bakel. "Perhaps it has," he said cautiously.

"If you know something, please tell me," said Romarda plaintively. "I am first of all a scientist, and my loyalty to the Congregation is tenuous and frankly dependent on my freedom to do research. The sum of recent events has suggested some metascientific advance that has eluded us."

"I hope you will visit me again, Jurse Romarda," said Bakel in an even tone, not dismissing him but leaving the question open, realizing that Romarda had bared a treasonous mind-set.

Romarda focused on Bakel and decided to leave it at that. "I will certainly do that, Allfather Bakel."

He exited and made for the stairway down. Sidestepping two Guardians as he rounded the corner, he approached the stairs. Pausing, he peeked back to see the Guardians halt at Bakel's door. After a short exchange with the guard, they were admitted. Not long after, Bakel emerged in restraints and was hustled back in his direction.

They aren't waiting. They have decided to cleanse him, thought Romarda as he scampered down the stairs. He found concealment as the stairway bottomed out and watched as the pair passed by, their captive in tow.

They will use the Cleansing Chamber in the temple for it, because it is most convenient. I must do something.

Romarda followed the trio, ducking behind pillars and remaining in the shadows. Circling the service area, he approached the Cleansing Chambers from the rear. A control panel with an array of blinking lights signaled the standby status of the apparatus. Only a thick velvet hanging separated it from the altar area so that any audible cue by the presiding priest could initiate action by the technician.

Romarda quickly removed the panel covering the circuitry, selected some leads, and jerked them free. Lifting the velvet curtain slightly, the Guardians could be seen placing a struggling Bakel in the Cleansing Chamber. The doors were closed, and one of the Guardians circled to approach Romarda's roosting place.

Trapped! . . . I will just have to play it out.

"Oh! Chief Romarda. We have orders to execute a Cleansing," one of the Guardians said.

"Yes, you will have to wait. I was just checking out a malfunction in the equipment. One of the recent . . . uh, demonstrations was somewhat incomplete."

The Guardian winced at the thought and circled to his partner still in the altar area with Bakel. Romarda heard the sound of low voices in consultation as he studied his frantic sabotage. He threw back the intervening curtain.

"I will need your help to get this thing up and running," said Romarda.

Bakel, now trussed up on the floor and consumed with terror, was stunned by the reappearance of Romarda, who was apparently in league with the Guardians. *It was all a plot to get me to reveal everything.*

Romarda ignored Bakel and addressed the Guardians. "The box in the upper corner of the chamber—take the cover off and tell me if there has been any arching."

"How can we tell?" said one.

"There will be some dark deposits in a localized area," said Romarda as he jerry-rigged the hastily severed leads.

"I don't see—" was all the Guardian got out. Romarda activated the Cleansing machine. A flash of light, not masked by closed chamber doors, filled the temple and momentarily blinded Bakel, whose vision cleared after a moment to reveal a surreal tableau. The two Guardians stood frozen in the act of doing something, a snapshot in time, one head turned as if commenting to his comrade, the other, pointing to some undefined issue.

Bakel gasped, still in shock as Romarda reappeared.

"We must get out of here," said Romarda, struggling with the Bakel's improvised bonds.

Dragging the dazed Allfather to the temple entrance, Romarda paused and looked out. *Nobody there . . . no worshipers or Guardians. The suppression is down, and everything is on hold till it can be restored.*

They slipped out the door and moved quickly down the temple main way as Bakel finally found his voice. "Wasn't that a bit extreme?" he asked. "Those men were just following orders."

"It was the only way," said Romarda. "It was them or us. If they had proceeded, you would be a statue. Now you must level with me. Are you or are you not in league with the insurgents?"

"What if I were? What could you do even if sympathetic?"

Romarda took a breath. "In spite of the lofty pronouncements of the Congregation concerning divine appointment and holy mission, they are dependent on the practical results of the pure science they so abhor in their doctrine. They have custody of them now but have no understanding of them, as can be seen by their absolute dependence on the DDS."

"Why all of a sudden have you realized this?" Bakel asked.

"Because having been left alone to explore what interests me most, the potential of pure science, it long ago reached a point of diminishing returns. I am late in realizing it. The appearance of enigmatic creatures from nowhere made me realize that my research has festered. What do you know about them?"

"I . . . don't know what you are talking about," said Bakel cautiously.

"They are part of the insurgency and have the Congregation and Ganderk in a tizzy. If you are part of it, you know about them. Now level with me. I saved your hide, didn't I?"

They hustled along silently, passed through the wall of trees, and turned right at the first crosswalk. Bakel spoke resolutely. "I will take you to a resting place, and you will wait."

Sensing he had made a breakthrough, Romarda said nothing.

The earthlings had just deactivated when the alarm indicated that someone was at the outer portal of the lab cover facility. Alaurenz quickly admitted the shaky and scuffed up Allfather Bakel.

"What happened?" he asked.

"They had me in confinement and were taking me for Cleansing when I was rescued by none other than Jurse Romarda himself. He wants to join us, or I think he does, but we must be aware of a trap. I took him to a place not in the direction of the lab, left him, and told him to wait. We must decide what to do. If he has truly turned, he would be of value to the cause."

"Maybe I should go talk to him and ferret out his motives. Maybe . . . make some kind of agreement," said Alaurenz.

Alaurenz and Bakel approached the lone figure resting on the park bench. Even seated, he presented a tall, stately appearance. Romarda rose as the two men approached.

"I fully understand your caution," he said breaking the ice. "You are rightly careful in any disclosures, but I am willing to do anything to gain you confidence."

"My name is Laurenz. So . . . why after serving the depraved of the Congregation have you decided to join us?" asked Alaurenz.

"I am first and foremost a scientist but am guilty of a myopic view of the world and have only of late summoned up the courage to resist it. My work has faltered under the strictures of the Congregation. I am particularly intrigued by the fully functioning holographic representations your scientific allies have fashioned to challenge the Congregation and the Guardians. I speak of both separately, because of late, the Guardians have shown a sign of taking over, since power unused has a way of surfacing. The Congregation thinks the Guardians operate at their behest, when in actuality the opposite is true. In reality, the Guardians, with Lauf Ganderk at the helm, are both a private army and a secret police—the worse possible combination. They can take over at any time, marginalize the Congregation, and put down any rebellion by force."

"Where are the soldiers of this army?" asked Alaurenz. "The Guardians locally seem limited in number, though enough to police and intimidate the populace."

"They can be quickly recruited in large numbers from the provinces. After all, the shutdown of the suppression broadcasts mostly affected Danvar. Many of the general policies and instructions are piped to the outlands so they have local control over the suppression," Romarda noted. "If your strategy is to start an insurrection here and have it spread, it may not work if you confine it to here. In a popular uprising, the Guardians could prevail with their superior weaponry. You will have to find a way that assures success."

"It is late," said Alaurenz finally. "Wait till dark, and I will have Bakel blindfold you and bring you to our base. I warn you—if this is a trick, we can memory erase you."

No response from Romarda signaled a deal. As darkness fell, Bakel led the blindfolded Romarda through back alleys and parks to the lab facility. Only an occasional curious passerby gave them a second look.

"Now," said Alaurenz, "you can see we are well equipped here. The grip of the Congregation has not hampered our progress. It has advanced hand in hand with the insurrection."

"I am impressed," said Romarda, blinking in the dazzle of the lab's artificial light. "By the looks of that instrument bank over there and the numerous chambers suggesting quantum manipulations, it is not surprising that you have come up with the lifelike surrogates that have so bedeviled the Congregation. There must be real-life counterparts. I assume they are members of your band, but I could not trace the origin of the controlling signal and would not have revealed it to the Congregation if I had I done so."

"Your speculations have a ring of truth," said Alaurenz. "But for now and pending further explanation, I am going to lock you up till I consult with my . . . uh, colleagues to decide what to do with you. You can join the Guardian we captured yesterday who was harassing our members. I will not bind you, but I warn that we have safeguards to prevent your escape."

"No danger of that," said Romarda. "I may already be on the blacklist when, along with my disappearance, Ganderk puts two and two together. As Allfather Bakel can attest, I had to cleanse two Guardians to extricate him."

The next day the earthlings assembled, transferred, and reinhabited their polymeric forms.

"I have a surprise," said Alaurenz. "The chief of the DDS has come to me to offer aid in our quest to overthrow the Congregation. He is still confined until I am thoroughly convinced that he is sincere and not a plant."

Alaurenz left and a few moments later returned with Romarda. "My friends, this is Jurse Romarda, chief scientist of the Diocese of Devine Science. He may or may not be aware that you are not real."

"Yes," said Romarda already confused by the appearance of Alaurenz' double. "I detect a faint shimmering, giving suspicion that they may be but representations of their real selves. Aside from this gentleman whom I see is by some mechanism a hologram of Laurenz who is standing here, I look forward to meeting them in the flesh. For now, it is my extreme pleasure to greet you in this spectral form, and I am humbled by the scope of man's knowledge, which has made it possible."

"Our pleasure is likewise," said Laurenz. "Unfortunately, you can only encounter our real selves if you are in the form you see—a hologram. Perhaps Alaurenz, my counterpart's designation for clarity, has not explained."

"First of all," Alaurenz began, "this man is not a holographic representation of me but that of my counterpart in another world. Did your research ever take you into the area of parallel worlds?"

"Only—only on paper, though I have speculated on it," gasped an astonished Romarda. *Perhaps at the wrong time and place,* he thought. "Such activity had to be approached with caution under restraints of the Congregation. That and many other areas of speculation are off limits because they conflict with their fundamental dogma, which assumes the uniqueness of this world. Don't tell me you have actually made contact."

"Better than that. Through our mutual efforts, I have visited there," said Alaurenz. "That is, I visited in the same form as the holograms that have come here to help us."

Romarda was speechless for a moment but finally spoke. "But . . . you are implying that the source world you have contacted is similar enough to our world that the inhabitants can pass from one to the other unnoticed. In the infinite number of possibilities, how can that be?"

"At this point, we do not know if there is an infinite number of worlds out there or just the one we have contacted," said Alaurenz, warming to the subject. "Offhand, the single parallel world makes little sense. To seize on a metaphor, what could cause a single fork in the road? We are left then with an unknown number of them. How can they be generated, unless at a precise moment driven by some yet unknown impulse, a new one is formed? We have posited that within the parameters of our universe, there may be a divergence at each plank interval, and a new universe is formed. Initially, it is a twin, but through time it develops significant differences. In this scenario, we have linked with this world because it is, in a sense, our closest relative."

"This is an overwhelming concept and reduces to insignificance our petty preoccupations," said Romarda. "So just what is this other world like?"

"Much like yours with the same problems demanding solutions," interrupted Laurenz. "We have in our history many regimes like the Congregation. Through the power of the people, they eventually succumbed. Though I have the impression that there is much more isolation here on Otherearth, less political and commercial interaction between nations and states. This would prolong the type of despotism we see here."

"Otherearth is it?" said Romarda, for the first time revealing a humorous side to his usual remote disengaged personality.

"Oh yes," said Alaurenz. "To lessen confusion, we have devised a whole vocabulary to distinguish between our Earth and theirs. For instance, by agreement, I am Alaurenz; he is

Laurenz, and so on. But to the task at hand, do you think your actions have compromised your credibility so that you are unable to blend back in?"

"I am not sure," said Romarda, again turning serious. "Nobody witnessed the Cleansing at the temple, so the Congregation may chalk it up to an accident, but the supposed cleansed Bakel has disappeared, and two Guardians are now statues. Ganderk is not naive and tends to be suspicious of unusual occurrences. The worst part of it is that he can and does act unilaterally. If he is pushed, he can wreak vengeance on anyone."

Alaurenz sat for a time twiddling his thoughts. "Okay, you can spend the day here and have free run of the facility. At nighttime, I will blindfold you again for safety and have one of us take you to a neutral place. I suggest you resume your normal duties till we see what kind of resistance is generated in the populace and decide on a future course."

XXI

Lauf Ganderk led a squad of Guardians into the DDS and spoke into the building's communication system. "I will be in charge here until further notice. Those of you who are idle because of the sabotage of the suppression broadcasts, go home until the techs have it up and running again."

Archfather Verkezian arrived soon after with robes aflutter and Allfather Leeche in tow. "This is outrageous. You are moving from your assigned place in the scheme to things. You will answer to the almighty for this futile action. And about these caravans of Guardians descending on Danvar from the provinces, is it part of your insolent attempt to grab power?"

"Quiet, priest!" Ganderk barked. "We have too long indulged you. For some reason, you think we have maintained the suppression for your pathetic goings on at the temple. I can tell you we only supported it because it kept things quiet. Go back to the temple and see if you can lure the herd back with you fanciful beliefs. Now leave, or I will confine you."

Verkezian stomped out, tailed by Leeche. They returned to the temple and hastily called a meeting of the Council. Red faced, Verkezian addressed those present. "I have just come from the DDS. Ganderk has . . . Where is everybody?" he said, eyeing the sparsely occupied room.

"Archfather, they are frightened," said Allfather Flecthrum. "The people are restless. So many of the Allfathers and sub prelates are deserting the temple and returning to their connections in the provinces. At this time, legions of Guardians are pouring into the city."

"At least they will keep people from marching on the temple," groaned a resigned Verkezian. "All right, we must button down, keep the temple closed until—"

"Archfather," cried Allfather Corvus, who had just arrived, "the Deacons who maintain the temple have told me that Allfather Bakel is missing, and two Guardians have been accidently cleansed. It is not known if the two incidents are related."

"That cements Bakel's guilt," said Verkezian. "He has been working with the insurgency all along and has been an informant planted among us. Does Ganderk know about the cleansed Guardians?"

"I don't know, but he will hit the ceiling when he hears of it and will blame us and the Holy Guard," said Corvus.

"Then dispose of the remains and put a muzzle on the Deacons," said Verkezian. "It will become just another mystery like the disappearance of that Guardian the other day."

The earthlings, along with Cralle and Janize, left to observe the state of things in Danvar.

"A lot of institutional activity has ceased, but essential services like transport and small business are still going strong," observed Laurenz.

"You would think it was a holiday, with kids playing and lots of laughter," said Marcia.

"Just what you would expect with the drag of the suppression lifted," said Cralle. "But I am beginning to see a lot of ominous black dots scattered about and in the distance. I am betting that Ganderk has summoned them from the provinces."

"I just hope nothing happens to that beautiful temple I visited," said Freda, who had remained quiet during the turbulence of recent events.

Christ, I had almost forgotten she was here, thought Laurenz as the others focused on her as someone who had appeared out of nowhere.

The group neared the neighborhood on the outermost side of the majestic wall of trees shielding the temple. The main way leading to the temple entrance was just ahead. They stopped short as Laurenz signaled. A group of Guardians was confronting a small gathering of citizens.

"Hold it here," said Laurenz. "That little get-together could turn nasty."

Low voices gradually rose in pitch with an accelerating pace of the back and forth. Suddenly, one of the participants was grabbed. As they attempted to take him away, others protested and were in turn taken into custody.

"It is just as I feared," said Cralle as all concentrated on the scene some fifty paces away, little noticing the shadow projected on the immediate foreground that was closing in on the action.

It was Freda.

"What's she doing?" asked Laurenz out loud, more to himself than the others.

"Freda!" Laurenz force whispered as she wafted forward.

"We need to stop her before she gets caught up in it," said Cralle as the others looked on in fascination.

"Fre—!" exploded Laurenz as Freda reached the scene of the altercation and spoke.

"Sirs, I am sure these good people meant no harm, and when tempers cool, apologies will be forthcoming," sang Freda.

"Away witch," growled one of the Guardians to the laughter of the others.

"But all good men respond to reason. If given a chance—"

Losing patience, the first Guardian advanced on the helpless Freda and whirled her around. The unexpected happened.

Though in her form Freda could only move with some three-quarters of normal speed, with precise mechanics, she levered the Guardian upward, arcing through the air to land in heap to the side.

"Oh my!" she proclaimed to the heavens and to the subdued Guardian. "Violence is so abhorrent. Let me help you up."

"Holy mother," cried Christian as the others looked on in disbelief. "She used judo on them. Or . . . it was more like Tai Chi speeded up with a vengeance. She must have learned that from the Shaolin."

The dismay of the other Guardians didn't last long. As Freda moved to the aid of the fallen Guardian, the others advanced and attempted to secure her. But Freda, compelled by a more basic instinct, responded in kind. The first to engage became locked in an arm-head grip, while the others clustered around and tried to unwind the amorphous blob presented by the two interlaced bodies. The lack of weight in her polymeric form, little more than half her real weight, was no impediment. In the struggle, she was continually lifted from the ground but remained fixed to the Guardian like a quadruped barnacle. One of the Guardians had retrieved a small weapon and was preparing to use it but was prevented by constant movement of the diversified tangle of Freda and the Guardian.

At some unknown signal, Christian, Laurenz, and Cralle rushed to Freda's defense. A brawl of considerable proportions ensued and ended with the armed guard flattened by Cralle's weapon and the others subdued and limping off.

"Oh my goodness, those poor, misguided creatures," said Freda.

"This is the first time I have used my judo in a real-life situation," said Christian as Cralle and Laurenz brushed themselves off. "It was weird lacking optimum speed and counterweight, but the principles of attack are the same without it."

Cralle, the only one of the lot in his real form, was only slightly scuffed up. For the first time, Laurenz noticed that a crowd had gathered and was glaring menacingly at several Guardians seen hovering at a safe distance in agitated conversation.

"Ganderk can bring out weapons now," said Cralle. "He cannot let it get out of hand. We must find some way to maintain momentum before the populace is cowered again."

"Perhaps the best way forward is to neutralize the Guardian headquarters itself," said Laurenz.

"I was thinking the same thing," said Cralle. "From the looks of this crowd, they are in no mood to be ruled by proclamation. If we can keep the suppression down, they will take care of the streets."

"How should we approach it?" asked Laurenz before turning and addressing Cralle. "You might know that, but you best not go with us. You are vulnerable."

"If you are taking on the headquarters, you are probably right," said Cralle. "But the place is locked down and unknown. I will go with you as far as the entrance. Then you will have to improvise. The problem is there are only two of you," he added, eying Laurenz and Christian.

"Maybe three," said Laurenz with a wink and nod at Freda.

"How about me?" protested Marcia.

"No way," said Laurenz again beset by vague fears concerning Marcia. "Besides, we need someone to bring Alaurenz up to date. You and Janize go back to the lab, report, and cool your heels."

Christian could be seen calming Janize, whose animated gestures revealed her disquiet at the prospect of his facing the Guardian stronghold.

"It's okay. They can't hurt me," said Christian.

"If everybody is ready," said Laurenz impatiently, "maybe we can get started. Coming, Freda?"

"Well, I don't know," said Freda, uncommonly sober. "I don't like violence, but this enterprise seems to invite it. I am not convinced that the problems cannot be resolved by peaceful means."

"Maybe you can just tag along and see if your approach works," said Laurenz nonchalantly, now aware that she reacted viscerally to events as they evolved.

"They what?" shouted Ganderk. "Let a woman and a bunch of bystanders overcome them? What kind of weeping willows do we have in the Guardian Corps? We have given them freedom from the suppression, and this is the level of service they give us?"

"They have too long been unopposed and have become soft," droned Jarbroak, his over active jowls undulating fiercely.

"They still have training, so there is no excuse for it," growled Ganderk.

"Yes, but with so long meeting little or no opposition, they have become a token force, only good for show," said Jarbroak. "They can spot irregularities but turn anemic when it comes to enforcement. Just look at what has happened in the last few days. One of our men got zapped in the middle of the procession to the temple, another has disappeared, and a team of our brightest was unable to prevent a shutdown of the suppression power source. The riffraff from the provinces are even less effective."

"Sir!" interrupted a Guardian who had just arrived. "It happened earlier, and it took some time to sort it out, but the two men who were sent to deal with Allfather Bakel have been cleansed at the temple. It may have been an accident, but Bakel is missing."

"Arm the troop, and to hell with Bakel and the rest of the Congregation," snapped Ganderk. "We will see who rules the Confederation."

The three earthlings and Cralle approached the Guardian headquarters to the accompaniment of Freda's steady drone of complacency and accommodation.

"I do hope we can avoid the same kind of misunderstanding we just had. Those men in the handsome black suits could have at least given us a chance to explain our mission here. If we can get—"

"Freda, you simply have to recognize evil when you see it," said Laurenz at pains to be pleasant. "All men are not motivated by love for fellow man and cannot be persuaded to it. We are pleasantly surprised that at some primal level you became aware of it." *Maybe that will shut her up.*

"But—" Freda started to say.

"Hold it," said Cralle as they rounded a corner and faced the imposing structure housing the Guardians. "Is that Ganderk?"

Lauf Ganderk, who had just exited the Guardian headquarters, turned and was hastening in a direction at right angles to their approach.

"He appears to be alone," mumbled Laurenz, his thoughts mirroring Cralle's unspoken ones. "He's headed in the direction of the DDS building and probably wants check on progress in efforts to reimpose the suppression."

"Shall we?" said Cralle.

"Why not?" said Laurenz as the group backtracked, cut into a side street, and raced to intercept the leader of the Guardians.

"Here he comes," said Cralle, peeking around a corner to see the truculent figure of Ganderk striding across the open space in front of the DDS.

"This is our chance. Let's go," said Cralle.

"No! Wait. Look—there and over there" said Laurenz, pointing. "Guardians, and they appear to be armed."

Several of the black-clad figures perked up as Ganderk approached and entered the DDS building.

"What do we do now?" asked Christian, who had said nothing since the altercation involving Freda.

"We can wait a little, but if he stays in there too long, we will need to deactivate and return to it tomorrow," said Laurenz, his impatience showing. "You know this is weird. It's like having a nine-to-five job as a guerilla."

"Yes, and your wife says cheerfully, 'How was your day dear?'" said Christian to the laughter of the others.

Ganderk entered the DDS and spoke to a technician. "When can you have the suppression signal back up?"

"Sir," explained the tech, "we are working on the problem, but there is a vacuum of leadership here at the DDS since Mr. Romarda has disappeared. It is not so much a matter of scientific know-how as one of logistics—who gives and signs off on the orders."

"Fix it!" yelled Ganderk as he stomped out.

"There he is again, and he's coming this way," said Cralle. "No . . . he is turning back the way he came. We must intercept him before reaches the Guardian headquarters."

They scurried along a side street parallel to Ganderk's route.

"Damn, he is going to get there before we can grab him," said Laurenz as Ganderk broke into the square in front of the headquarters building whose entrance was punctuated by the random in-and-out flow of Guardians.

"Shall we?" said Cralle, removing his stunner from a pocket.

"No," said Laurenz slowly. "You can move fast, but we can't. If we try to take him in such a public place, half the headquarters will storm out in his defense. We would be overwhelmed in flight. We must do it another way. Let's fade back into the artery that brought us here and wait for a stray Guardian or two to wander past. If we can don a couple of those black getups, maybe we can just walk in. From there, we will have to improvise."

The four moved back into the maze of buildings and stood vigilant in one of the doorway insets. It was not long before a group of Guardians was seen approaching.

"How about now?" said Cralle.

"Too many," said Laurenz. "We have to think about what to do with the bodies after we capture them, so two is the maximum."

The Guardians passed by, giving scarce attention to the earthlings who had paired off and feigned relaxed conversation. A few moments later a single Guardian was seen coming their way. Laurenz gave Cralle the high sign. Cralle turned as the Guardian passed and gave him a dose from his stunner. Laurenz caught him as he fell. They dragged him into a secluded walk space and began to strip him.

"Oh my!" exclaimed Freda wide-eyed when the Guardian was found to have no underwear.

"Give him an extra dose," said Laurenz as the Guardian began to stir. He then addressed Christian. "See if you can get into that; it's more your size. Now we need another one."

Several moments passed, during which the Guardians seemed to only exit in groups. Finally, a lone figure was seen coming their way.

They neutralized him in the same manner as the first, and soon Laurenz and Christian stood side by side like a pair of expectant crows waiting for comment.

"Well?" said Laurenz.

"Yours is a little baggy but convincing enough," said Cralle finally, suppressing a grin.

"Okay," said Laurenz. You and Freda truss up these two with anything you can find, while Christian and I see what we can do in the Guardian's lair. Cralle, lend me your stunner. Of course, we cannot use it on Ganderk, since we would have nothing but a limp body should we have to make a hasty exit.

For now, I think you and Freda should join Marcia and Janize back at the lab."

The group separated. Laurenz and Christian made their way toward the Guardian headquarters.

"Here goes nothing," mumbled Laurenz as they passed through security with little more than a nod from the guard. "Now, which way? We couldn't hope to consult a directory, because anybody who is even allowed in here knows where he is going and where he belongs."

"How about that elevator?" said Christian, pointing. "We can do a token survey of the floors, as the door opens on each level."

They entered the elevator and just as the doors were about to close, two Guardians rushed in. Christian and Laurenz exchanged glances as the lift rose to the upper floors.

"Floor?" said one of the Guardians to Laurenz as the elevator came to a stop.

"What?" said a startled Laurenz.

"You forgot to press your floor," said the Guardian.

"Oh . . . uh, nine, and thank you."

The Guardian started to press the number but hesitated. "It won't stop there. It's the Chief's floor. Only his key permits it."

"Oh, for heaven's sake, I must have been dreaming. I meant ten," said Laurenz fingering the stunner.

"That's the vestibule leading to the roof. What's going on up there?" said the Guardian as the other one now took note of the exchange.

"It's . . . a new setup for surveillance. Want to come up and see?" quickly responded Laurenz under pressure to display firm purpose.

"No, we are in somewhat of a—"

"Why not," interrupted the second Guardian.

The rest of the assent occurred in silence. As they reached the top, Laurenz casually motioned the two Guardians to exit. As they cleared the lift's portal, Laurenz applied the stunner to the most rearward of the two. He silently sagged to the floor, but the thud caused the front most to turn.

"Wha—" was all he got out before Laurenz doused him with the stunner.

They dragged the two bodies out of sight under the ascending stairway leading to the roof.

"Look around. See if there is something to bind and gag these two. I don't know how long they will be out."

Christian probed the recesses of the space, which was apparently a dumping ground for antiquated and dysfunctional equipment.

"Here—this wire is just the thing," said Christian from a corner gathering handfuls of it. "We can bend it around, and it will act just like handcuffs."

"Yeah—oh good, long and short pieces. Stick a stretch of it through their mouths and bind it at the back of the head," said Laurenz. "Otherwise, they will come to and start yelling to high heaven."

"What a break," said Laurenz. "We know now that Ganderk is parked on the ninth floor." With the two Guardians trussed up, he considered and then put a short segment of the wire in his pocket. *This may come in handy.*

"We can't enter that floor from the elevator, so how can we get to him?" asked Christian.

"Well . . . it's about a floor and a half from the roof. We are lucky the Guardian inadvertently revealed it. Maybe we can reach it from there. See if there is something resembling a rope in that pile of rubble," said Laurenz, pointing to the clutter at one end of the enclosure.

Christian inspected the pile and pulled on the end of another strip of wire protruding from the mess. "It's stuck, but there is more rolled up in back behind this dead machine. Just a minute, I think I can reach it," he said straining.

"Good," said Laurenz as he inspected the find, a considerable length of thick, insulated wire. "Since we weigh less, it should hold us fine if we use it separately. Let's take a look at the roof."

"Okay, but what do you have in mind?" asked Christian.

"Something outrageously flamboyant, if you are up to it."

"I am afraid to ask."

"Come on," said Laurenz as they scampered up to the roof.

Laurenz peered over the edge, revealing a courtyard far below and, from his perspective, an ordered array of windows descending in columns of ever-diminishing trapezoids. They circled the yawning space and inspected the windows for any kind of movement.

"Not much going on there," said Laurenz. "Looks more or less deserted, but we can't count on it. Ganderk's nook is probably on the corner of the building. You know, the old executive's office privilege. Best we enter from here, however."

Returning to the side above Ganderk's office, Christian asked, "Should we tie off and lower ourselves?"

"No, a George of the Jungle maneuver will give us surprise and lessen the chance we will be seen from the floors below."

"George of what?" Christian questioned.

"Cartoon character before your time—and mine too but prominent in the archives."

"Okay, but just how will it work?" asked Christian in a skeptical monotone.

"We will choose a window as an entry point and tie off right above it with the other end attached around our waists. I will go first, because I have some experience in this. I will back up and run as fast as possible toward the edge. It will take me out into the space, but the rope will catch as I fall and arc me into the side of the building, hopefully with a bull's-eye on the window. I will lock my feet together to minimize the area and maximize the force at the point of contact with the glass. Hopefully, when you follow after me, the window should be more or less missing."

"You have got to be kidding," squeaked a befuddled Christian. "And experience? What experience?"

Verging in the comic, a serious Laurenz responded. "Oh, didn't I tell you? That's the way I escaped from the DDS building after totaling the antenna. Only in that case, just I dived off the roof. This maneuver is more intricate."

"But—"

"All I did was bounce, although I'll have to admit it was scary. There was a little dent in my fill, but otherwise I was intact. You are so used to this form you forget we really can't be harmed. Now let's get on with it."

Laurenz secured the wire at the top and flopped it over the edge for measurement. *Thaaat—should be about right.* He marked the wire and with some difficulty severed it. Negotiating a similar length for Christian, he again tied it off.

"Tie it around your waist like this and then slide the knot to the back." Before Christian had a chance to object, he continued. "Okay, stand to the side. When you hopefully hear the crash, follow in about five seconds."

Laurenz backed up and raced as fast as his form could permit toward the edge. He disappeared as gravity took over, and he hurdled in an arc toward the courtyard below. Finally the rope caught, and he curved toward the side of the building. He found himself flailing blindly for orientation, as he was facing away from the end of his trajectory. Luck was with him even though it was not the graceful Olympic form of a diver with which he struck the window. In a split second, he managed only a half twist but remained vertical so that the encounter was full on, further mangling the facial portion of his fill. The window shattered along with the portions of the frame.

A few seconds later, Christian sailed quietly through the newly made opening with a grin on his face.

"How did you do that?" growled a disgruntled Laurenz as he picked shards of glass from his polymeric form.

"I kept the knot in front so when the wire came taut, it snapped me around."

"I suppose that noise will wake up the dead," said Laurenz, still piqued at his bad choice. He peered out and below from the splintered opening where the window was. "No, we seem to have managed it without alerting the other floors."

"Yes, but Ganderk must be on this floor," said Christian. "Surely he—"

"What's going on here? You two are from maintenance? What kind of incompetence could cause such damage? Get out of here. This is a restricted area."

Laurenz and Christian gaped at Ganderk. *He doesn't realize who we are*, thought Laurenz as he and Christian compelled by coordinated inspiration advanced on Ganderk.

Ganderk instantly recognized his error and retreated toward the recesses of the floor.

"After him, and stay between him and the elevator," said Laurenz. "Only he can call it from this floor. If he reaches it, we are trapped here."

"He didn't go that way," said Christian as he raced after the fleeing Ganderk. "He is probably headed for his office to call for help. We can run him down, but it will take both of us to secure him."

The limitations of their forms permitted only a loping cadence. They could only keep up but not overtake the ungainly Ganderk even though he moved at only a modest speed. He rounded a corner with Ganderk still some thirty feet ahead. An open door lay ahead with a view of outside beyond. Ganderk burst through the door, slammed it shut, and could be heard fumbling with the lock. Without slowing, the combined weight of Christian and Laurenz slammed into the door. It gave, because Ganderk could not secure it quickly enough. They stood glaring at Ganderk who glared back.

"You are trapped here," Ganderk said. "How would you expect to escape? My men will be all over you."

"Watch him," said Laurenz as he inspected the room. The office, otherwise Spartan, was filled with the minimal electronics needed to control the populace and doubtless to check on his own men. "That balcony outside the sliding doors is one of his perks. We may be able to use it."

"How is that?" asked Christian. The same question was on the rattled face of Ganderk.

"Leave him in the corner over there and come here," said Laurenz.

Christian moved to where Laurenz was standing. Laurenz whispered into his ear for some thirty seconds, while Ganderk stood seething. Christian glanced toward the doors and back at Laurenz.

"Do you think it will work?" asked Christian.

"I'm sure of it," said Laurenz, his tone not quite matching the confidence of his words."

Laurenz and Christian moved on Ganderk, who shrank at the sheer determination of their advance. They grabbed the trembling chieftain and penguin walked him to and through the doors to the teetering edge of the balcony with only a low railing separating them from the emptiness.

"I'll take him from behind, and you embrace him at the front," said Laurenz as the two encapsulated their trembling charge.

"What is this?" said Ganderk in a gasp of lucidity, momentarily freed by bizarre actions of his captors. "Some kind of perverse sexual behavior you insurgents indulge in?"

"Shut up. Duck your head in and curl up your legs," snapped Laurenz. "Let's just hope we don't land head first.

"Wha," sniveled Ganderk when with Laurenz' nudging, the compacted trinity toppled over the edge.

The silent descent was broken only by the frantic whimper of Ganderk. Unable to adjust their position, they were at the mercy of the initial forces of their launching and the vagaries of the atmosphere. They met the ground in a more or less horizontal position. Laurenz' back made contact with the ground first. He and Christian held on as the threesome bounced chaotically and finally settled. They released the traumatized Ganderk who sagged in relief to hug the ground, which promised sanctuary from the interminable moment of acrophobia he had just experienced.

"How does it look from the back?" asked Laurenz as he inspected himself. "Flattened, with the imprint of my also flattened hands and forearms rather comical," said Christian, now recovered from the experience.

"Yeah, we'll both need a tune-up if we ever make it back to the lab. For now, we need to get Ganderk away from here before he is recognized or we run into a bunch of Guardians."

A few random passersby did witness the outlandish episode—not the fall but the strange gyrations of the three at the end.

"If they don't look too close, they will see us as Guardians on some mission," said Laurenz as he gave the witnesses the once-over.

A few onlookers stood scattered and at some distance starred in disbelief. One by one, they looked away, a holdover from the yoke of the suppression where no one involved themselves in the affairs of the Guardians.

They gathered up the still wide-eyed Ganderk, who had craned his neck to look to the heights from which they had fallen. Securing his hands with the extra wire he had taken, Laurenz considered. "Do you have a handkerchief in one of the pockets? We should put together a blindfold. That will hide his identity from any close scrutiny and prevent his knowing where we are taking him."

"Yes. Here's one," said Christian.

Laurenz fashioned a make-do blindfold, and they dragged him away, keeping to the parkland behind the Guardian headquarters, which bordered the heavily congested area of their initial approach.

Plunging back into the network of cross streets and thickly settled neighborhoods, they made their way unchallenged back to the lab. They paused at the entrance of the building that served as a front for the clandestine lab.

"I hope Alaurenz doesn't panic at the sight of us dressed as Guardians and will take a closer look," said Laurenz.

After an extended wait, the door clicked open. Alaurenz greeted them with weapons and several beefy members of the crew. He heaved a sigh of relief as he recognized his two compatriots.

"What happened to you?" asked Alaurenz, appraising Laurenz' beat up face. "I see you have had a busy day. And who is that behind the mask?"

"None other than the flesh-and-blood Ganderk," said Laurenz. "His retention should cut the heart out of the Guardian response."

"Well, well, it is Mr. G himself," Alaurenz said. "I won't ask how you pulled it off."

"Yes. Don't ask," said Laurenz as he twisted around, presenting a view from the rear. "Maybe you can fix us up with new fills."

Alaurenz burst out laughing. "That is the weirdest thing I have ever seen."

"If you think that's weird, get a load of these leafy arms," said Christian as he held out his battered appendages now peeled away, revealing the more ephemeral outline of his holographic form.

"Hustle the chief in," said Alaurenz, recovering his accustomed sobriety. "He can keep his underling company in our makeshift cell. You are no doubt tired and want to deactivate. I will alter the portal settings for you two, so you can return as holograms, and I can give you new fills. Let's join the others."

Threading their way past the enormous front machine and through the locker doorway, they entered the lab. Janize ran to

Christian and embraced him. He responded in kind with his still-filmy appendages. The others turned away but not before Marcia gave Laurenz her famous worried look.

Alaurenz spoke to one of the lab techs. "Take Ganderk down to the cell and secure him. We will interrogate him later."

A still-blindfolded Ganderk muttered something inaudible to the shrugs of Laurenz and Christian.

"Okay," said Laurenz. "Let's all park and deactivate."

XXII

Laurenz emerged from the chamber and met with the others. "I need to get to the gym and work these kinks out."

"I'll go too," said Christian. "I'm not used to staying immobile for such a length of time."

"It's a swim for me and a brisk walk to get my weight-bearing legs back," said Marcia.

"Okay, then meet me at Mario's at, say . . . seven. Where's Freda?" asked Laurenz suddenly realizing she wasn't there.

"She must still be in the chamber," said Laurenz. "But I don't know about rousing her. We don't know the effect of involuntary deactivation. If she stayed, Alaurenz will deal with her."

Alaurenz turned away to close the lab down for the day, and the techies had retired to their respective abodes, except for a few who stayed to assure the security of the captives.

"You cannot just leave things to settle themselves alone," said Freda, who had suddenly appeared as out of nowhere.

With a twitch, Alaurenz responded. "Oh—Freda, you startled me. I thought you were deactivating with the others."

"I was but thought the better of it. I have been thinking about your approach to ridding Danvar of what I have come to understand are evil forces that repress the people."

"Yes?" said Alaurenz expectantly.

"It has no political element, no interaction with those who would rise up, and most importantly, no leaders," said Freda. "Your hopes that it will spontaneously generate by itself if you create the right conditions are excessively optimistic."

Alaurenz remained silent but focused on Freda with renewed interest. "What do you suggest?"

"My organization back on Earth, The United Mystics Coalition, has considerable experience in motivating a docile citizenship to action."

"It is late. What can you do at this very moment?"

"This is the time, after a day's work, when the people get together in various settings for social and recreational purposes. We can start by intruding on these, in a friendly way, of course. Surely, the lifting of the suppression has not only broadened the scope of their activities but has become a topic of general discussion. Perhaps you can tell me where these places of assembly are."

"Well . . . there are the social clubs and the trade guilds for a starter. But what would you do? Just walk in and start ranting?"

"I could try. Perhaps you could point me to one of the guilds. There is usually a reservoir of pent-up testosterone in men of gruff trade pursuits that is itching to express itself. Now that the suppression is down, all that is needed is the right stimulus."

This should be interesting to watch, thought Alaurenz, somewhat amused. "I'll do better that and take you over to the Guild of Machine Operators, which usually meets on this night once a week. We will see how they respond to your . . . uh, presentation."

Freda and Alaurenz left the lab and journeyed back toward the center of the city. A gruff gray building with see-through glass doors and a lit foyer revealed working man types milling around. Beyond was a door opening to a larger space. "Good," said Alaurenz, appraising the scene. "There are women present too, probably wives, girlfriends, and relatives of the workers. This will make us less conspicuous. The get-togethers are usually half social and half business."

They melted into the crowd and entered the meeting hall. Small groups were chatting seriously. From what Alaurenz could hear, the newly acquired freedom was the chief topic of conversation, but there seemed to be a difficulty in expressing it, as if a compulsion always considered part of their own volition was now gone.

The meeting seemed about to start so Freda and Alaurenz sat down.

With the bang of a gavel, a burly man with white hair began to speak. "We all assemble here in a mood of unaccustomed abandon. We all knew that something was manipulating us with caps on our ability to participate in the government and laying on us unexplained urges like the timed visits to the temple. For some reason, the source of the restraints and compulsions is now gone."

"That explosion at the Diocese of Devine Science has something to do with it," interrupted one of the workers to the murmured ascent of his fellows. "I'm sure of it."

Freda is right, thought Alaurenz. *They have only a vague idea of what has been happening. It must be ex—*

"Let's hope it stays this way," continued the speaker, intruding on Alaurenz' thoughts. "We—"

Freda's voice cut through the din, "If I may interrupt, your comrade is right, but you don't seem to realize that the Congregation, through the technology and the enforcement wing of Guardians has purposefully and with evil intent levied this burden upon you."

The assembly, unaccustomed a woman expressing herself in the meeting hall, turned in a body to focus on Freda.

"The relief from suppression is only temporary unless you and others like you take to the streets and assert the power of the people," continued Freda.

"But the Guardians are the police of Danvar, and lately we have noticed an increase in their numbers," said the white-haired leader. "What can we do?"

"Do you think that their increased presence is a coincidence?" asked Freda. "It obviously has to do with the lifting of the suppression. If you wish to retain your newly found freedom, you must incite your fellow citizens and march on the seats of power."

"But they have weapons," someone moaned.

"If you act in unison, you vastly outnumber and will intimidate them into restraint of their use. There is a risk, but you must do it now or suffer the consequences. You must marshal your fellow guilds and other groups and move quickly," concluded Freda as she signaled Alaurenz to leave.

Eyes followed Freda as they exited. From outside, they saw within the coalescence of small groups followed by a mass exit from the meeting hall.

Alaurenz, dumbfounded by what had just taken place, gazed at Freda with renewed respect. "You were right. Not only were they scarcely aware of what was happening to them, but they had no idea what to do. We will see what tomorrow brings."

It was late when Freda and Alaurenz returned to the lab.

"I will retire to the group's resting place and deactivate," said Freda. "I am sure the others wonder where I am."

The next day all the earthlings assembled except Freda.

"Late again," said Laurenz, somewhat disgusted. "We will go this time without her."

"Wait a minute," said Christian. "Maybe she never returned and is still in the chamber."

"Not there," said Nate, who had just entered. "She got back around ten o'clock last night and went home."

"Okay," said Laurenz after a pause and somewhat irritated. "If she can manage it and show up, send—"

"Sorry I'm late," said Freda, appearing suddenly and looking a little tired. "I stayed longer last night to try something else to help the insurgency."

No, don't ask, Laurenz thought to himself.

The group transferred and once again inhabited their fills. As they strode toward the center of the lab, Alaurenz could be seen facing another figure, which seen in profile presented faint glow and a disquieting familiarity. As they neared, Alaurenz turned toward them, his face blanched with an unreadable expression. The other figure also turned and spoke.

"My name is Laurenz Kapro. I have come here by means of—" He paused as he recognized himself approaching. There followed an embarrassing moment where none of the three Kapros could move himself to speak.

"Well now, aren't we in a pickle?" said Marcia, breaking the spell and entertaining for the first time the fleeting thought, *I wonder if there are other versions of me?*

Alaurenz emerged from his stupor. "There are three of us now. We appear to be insulated from one another by the nature of the process that links us, but lingering is an escalation of questions to haunt us. How many more variations of us are there? And are they all benign, or are some hostile?"

The differences between Laurenz and Alaurenz, with the exception of their hair (or lack thereof), were minimal. They both had the same facial and body features. The resemblance to the third Laurenz stopped there. He was a lean version in oddly ornate dress, a bizarre mixture evoking at the same time both rococo and art deco. The featured well-fitting, tunic-style jacket was conventional enough, but the overlay of Egyptian-esque applique with an abbreviated ruffle peeking out from both the sleeves and collar, along with tapered trousers of charcoal color that disappeared into a low rise boot, skewed the image.

He's got to be kidding, thought Laurenz.

"We probably need first to know how the Mr. Kapro before us was able to get here," said Laurenz of Earth, catching himself and finding his own voice. "Then maybe we can figure out how many more may try and if they are all as mutually benign as we seem to be."

"Now that I am confronted with the reality of yet another world and a jolting set of triplicate likenesses, I see what you are getting at," said Alaurenz.

"For our part, we were exploring numerous avenues relating to disturbances at quantum level," said Laurenz, addressing the newcomer. "It was most surprising that one of our lesser efforts has borne fruit, involving an odd effect resulting from the successive bounce of images using mirrors in opposition. Then it became evident that by some device, someone from somewhere was able to inject an image in the seventh of the series. Most disconcerting, the image was that of my counterpart here and a near duplicate of me. And so, my simmering friend, it took a response from him, who by agreement we call Alaurenz, to devise a method to insert fully functioning holographs of ourselves back into the series. It appears that the mirror arrangement once in place can demonstrate the effect universally. It is left for alternate worlds to discover it. As of now, whether many or only specific alternate Earths can be linked is unknown."

"I apologize for my scintillate feature," said the third Laurenz with a touch of humor. "I see you have been able to eliminate it and, in addition, impart solidity to your form. Regarding the primitive probe you spoke of, we did receive it in the form of an indistinct image. Perhaps we did not have the appropriate detection devices in place."

"You have now given us at least a small increment in our understanding of the phenomenon," said Laurenz. "We ourselves discontinued our own primitive transmissions after we made contact with Laurenz here on his Earth, believing the link was unique. It appears we were a bit premature in that. But if no more like you show up, we may have exhausted the potential of like worlds to link. In any case, cosmic forces are at play, and we haven't the foggiest idea of what they are."

A period of reflection seemed to settle over the trio of Laurenzes as the others stood by in various states of awe. It was left to Freda to break the silence.

"What are the features of spiritual life on your world?" she asked.

"The spirit?" said the third Laurenz, caught unaware by the change of subject but responding with a question. "You perhaps mean religion. It's quite institutionalized and under government control—to a point."

"I guess you could say the same for Earth," said Laurenz, picking up the thread.

"By spiritual, I was referring to a more general attitude toward the unearthly and nonmaterial," persisted Freda.

"Oh, we have our numerous cults and radical offshoots of the mainstream," said the third Laurenz lightly to Freda's annoyance of his choice of words.

"How about interaction between governments?" asked Alaurenz. "Is there any?"

"Yes, of course," said the third Laurenz. "How could world commerce and other international entities function without it?"

"True. Here we manage it, but at great price," said Alaurenz. "Our Otherearth, dubbed thus for convenience, until now has been divided into two main religious autocracies, which by common agreement do not interact, believing that it will lead to inevitable conflict and mutual destruction. This part of the world, consisting of the north and south continents of Columbus, has been controlled by The Devine Congregation of Infinite Wisdom and Compassion. By strange coincidence and due to action just completed, that is beginning to change.

"In the combined continents to the east, it is as bad or worse. The Assembly of Moslem Clerics holds sway backed up by the Holy Army of the Great God Allah. They shun any interaction in fear of losing power. Only the small continent of Australia to the south of the equator possesses anything like the governing system of your worlds. But to the matter at hand, we on this Earth were motivated to interworld contact not only for scientific quest, but because of a crisis in our local situation. This very facility we inhabit is secret and clandestine because of the danger from the authorities. It is also the center of an insurgency. Laurenz here of Earth and his companions have with the incentive of continuing contact agreed to help lift the yoke of tyranny that suppresses us. Unless you can help, you are just in the way," he added bluntly.

This place is a hodgepodge of similarities and dissimilarities with Earth, thought Laurenz as he listened fascinated at Alaurenz' narrative, realizing that in the rush to resolve the local situation, he had little grasp of the overall cultural, geographic, political, and religious issues on the rest of Otherearth.

"At the moment, I cannot see how we—" began the third Laurenz.

"Perhaps he can," said Laurenz, interrupting. "What is the state of the enforcement resources in your world?"

"Each country has its own at all levels," said the third Laurenz.

"Is there any small group, preferably secret, that works covertly?" asked Laurenz.

"Not really . . . well, yes. It is rarely called upon and held in disrepute by many, but it has support in high places because of its effectiveness in situations where nothing else has worked. Its mode of operation is through the occult."

"That's all we need," said Alaurenz with a sneer, "adding a bunch of sorcerers to a corrupt society already based on fantasy."

"Do not underestimate the power of the metaphysical," said Freda, who had been following the exchange. "It motivates our group back on Earth even though we struggle for the authorities to take us seriously."

This is going in the wrong direction, thought Alaurenz, who, not wanting to fuel controversy, choked back his deep-seated reservations.

"How could they help?" asked Alaurenz with a blitheness reflecting sarcasm.

The third Laurenz hesitated. "I am not sure, because they work through spells."

Alaurenz winced. *Worse than I thought.*

"But not the metaphysical kind usually associated with the word," continued the third Laurenz, "but by a process more akin to mass hypnosis."

Laurenz' brow knit, and the others gazed at the floor or the sky. Freda, on the other hand, perked up.

"That's fascinating. I would love to see them in action," said Freda.

"Who is the leader, and do you think we could talk him into coming here? How would he fit into our overall strategy?" asked Alaurenz in a sardonic challenge to the ridiculous. "Our own people for the time being have just come out of the scientific equivalent of a spell. How could we use the same strategy to defeat the Congregation and the Guardians?"

"You imply some malevolent feature to the spell or whatever it was that afflicted you." said the third Laurenz. "Perhaps you could go talk to him. The leader of the group is Ernst Vascho. I would first have to explain to him the unusual circumstances of the mission, because nobody outside of a closed circle of scientists knows of our interworld breakthrough."

Alaurenz looked around. *I see blank faces and no apparent support against such a goofy idea, but Freda who stands there elated at the prospect of meeting a fellow kook.*

A puzzled Laurenz chimed in, addressing Alaurenz. "You may have to go alone. We are here in holographic form and can always return to our own world by just deactivating, but if any of us went this third alternate Earth, we would need to be relayed—that is, transshipped. Is this possible? Also, now that a link has been established between Otherearth with yet another Earth variant, does your technology differentiate the transfer from here back to our world and from that of the third Laurenz?"

"We can probably affect the transfer as we did with you through the link he made by coming here," said Alaurenz. "As for the transshipping of your holograms, we will have to wait for that science to develop. So you are right. For now, I shall have to engage this Ernst Vascho alone and what he has to offer. I will prepare for that while you and your group see if you can support the momentum of last night's activity, if you are willing."

"What was that?" asked Laurenz.

"An idea Freda had," said Alaurenz. "We went to the meeting hall of one of the guilds and roused them to action . . . we think."

"So that's where she was," said Laurenz, now entirely freed from any doubts as to what Freda might do.

Alaurenz' hologram stepped from the mirror enclosure and looked back. The mirrors from which he had emerged possessed a mystical quality. *Not glass, that's for certain,* thought Alaurenz. *It is some kind of metal or alloy. From that faint under glitter, they must be cast not drawn, and . . . thin as it is, how does it sustain the tension forces created by its own weight?*

His thoughts and attention to the oddities of yet another world were interrupted by the approach of the real-life, flesh-and-blood third Laurenz. "Welcome to Earth, uh . . . Alaurenz."

Even weirder than his hologram, thought Alaurenz as he appraised his Earth three real-life visitor. *Every perceived anomaly of before is now exaggerated.*

Alaurenz looked around. The lab technicians were dressed and coiffured basically the same as third Laurenz with allowances for some of the more rigorous duties required. *Okay, now where is this Ernst Vascho ding-a-ling?*

As if responding to Alaurenz' thoughts, Laurenz three said, "I have made contact with Vascho, and a meeting has been set up in early evening. You will go clothed, of course. The only hint of your strangeness will manifest itself in your exposed parts, which will be masked in the fading light."

The two alternate Laurenzes approached the outdoor café. A tall, thin man sipping coffee looked up and addressed the third Laurenz.

"Laurenz, what a pleasure to see you again. We haven't crossed since the conference on metaphysics," said Vascho, addressing him with a nod to Alaurenz. He then added without pause, "I see you have in some way linked with the beyond."

"Is it that obvious?" asked the third Laurenz while Alaurenz was flabbergasted at the Vascho's blasé response in the presence of his own proxy self.

"Considering the presence of your shimmering double and the request to see me in the first place, I conclude that you may have encountered a problem that perhaps only I can engage."

"Yes," said the third Laurenz. "My counterpart here comes from a society just liberated from a yoke of suppression imposed by way of a malevolent behavior-altering signal broadcasted to the populace. Unfortunately, the revolution, for want of a better word, is tenuous and may stall due to confusion, lack of focus in the affected masses, and the presence of the enforcement authority Alaurenz refers to as the Guardians."

"One way forward may be suggested by the mechanism used to subdue your people in the first place," said Vascho after a pause. "The same process can possibly be altered to instill a universal sense of brotherly love."

"We have had enough of being manipulated," broke in Alaurenz at the edge of his patience.

"I don't mean as a permanent condition," said Vascho. "But if behavior can be altered by a imposing a specific technology, it can be reprogrammed precisely to produce a different result."

"Changed in what way?" pressed an ever-skeptical Alaurenz.

"You imply that the process used to subdue your people is a tranquilizing one and suggests that only general features of the human psyche be manipulated. Perhaps it can be replaced with one of the same nature that instills a sense of hope and optimism. I am aware of your fears concerning mass hypnosis. My idea is more of a catharsis of the fears and suspicions that afflict all of us."

"So even if you could put the Guardians and corrupt clergy who subdue us under such a pall, who is to say that once it is lifted, they will not resort to their old behavior?" asked Alaurenz.

"They are surely vastly outnumbered by the populace as a whole," said Vascho. "Once liberated from the present restraints and given a period of respite to direct their own destiny, a new order should prevail. Beyond that, who is to say that there would not be a residual effect on the oppressors themselves? After all, beyond the corrupt leaders, the cadre assumes the day-to-day functions of the Guardians. Are they not recruited from a cross section of the population in the first place? Even though they compromised some accepted unethical principles to begin with, as many in life do, they will accept reality and conform."

"Yes, but as a practical matter, these local enforcers will be out of a job," said Alaurenz. "The citizenry will push the envelope if it comes to putting food on the table."

"Correct," said Vascho. "Although, they won't be out of a job permanently, because personnel are always needed to keep the public order. The transition will be rocky, but new leaders can redefine the parameters of law endorsement and public behavior."

Alaurenz stood silent. *It is a little vague, but it is at least a way forward that we hadn't considered before.* "Could you be persuaded to come to our world and assist in the process you have suggested? Of course, it will have to be in the same proxy form as I have used to come here, but you will retain all your creative capacity."

"It should be and new and transcendent experience," said Vascho.

"I will prepare a chamber of repose for Vascho and project his holo to Alaurenz' home Earth," said third Laurenz. "I will sequester and follow him."

A period lapsed, before arrangements could be made for the transfer. Upon their arrival to Otherearth, the two were greeted by real Alaurenz who had disengaged from his holographic form.

"Let us hope your plan works, because we have a tenuous situation here," said Alaurenz. "Please consult with our specialists, Cralle Damon and yet another version of myself, Laurenz Kapro, to whom being our first Otherearth contact we have awarded the un-prefixed appellation 'Laurenz.' You will, of course, notice that he is in holo form."

The novelty of it again asserted itself. As if seeing their counterparts for the first time, all once again gaped in wonder, except Vascho who seemed to take any departure from reality in stride. Alaurenz broke the trance.

"The becalming transmission is still down but only temporarily. Reports are that the primary egress of the channels carrying the signal to the provinces is being repaired and that locally a temporary transmitting facility is being reestablished atop the Guardian headquarters where the statue masking the antenna once stood. We must first figure out a way to take it all out for good."

XXIII

Alaurenz, Cralle, and the holos of the third Laurenz, Laurenz, and Christian sat pondering the best way forward. The holo form of the inscrutable Vascho spoke up.

"I think before considering an alternative becalming signal, we must first neutralize the present one for good," said Vascho. "You have indicated that each time you have compromised it they have managed to jerry-rig the thing back up, and they are obviously doing that now."

"Yes," said Alaurenz. "Once we do it, however, the other centers like Jarlink and Alderton will continue to broadcast the suppression independently, but they will be isolated in the sea of independent provinces. We can then deal with them one at a time. The liberated flow of news will undoubtedly accelerate the process."

"Any attempt to infiltrate the Guardian stronghold here by stealth is bound to fail, and we might have to abandon our holos in the process," said Laurenz. "Perhaps the only way would be to deposit us directly at the source of the signal. Even then, the uncertainty would remain. Could we do something to keep it down, and could we destroy it without totaling the personnel in the floors below?"

"How about a catapult to at least get us up there?" asked Christian.

"And just how would that work?" asked Cralle, at once overwhelmed by images of bodies hurling through space.

"Well, those of us in this form could maybe do it with little to lose if we failed," said Laurenz cautiously. "The question is, where would we launch from, and even if we could get there, how could we take out the transmission for good?"

They descended into silence until Vascho spoke up. "What if you got some radioactive material and contaminated the whole site. The personnel would have time to abandon the place? That would not only put down the transmission site and make it unusable, but also force evacuation of the Guardian headquarters."

"Someone would actually have to get in there and scatter the stuff around," said Laurenz. "In this form, I could handle it without being harmed, although I would have to abandon my contaminated holo someplace like I did before."

Cralle turned to Alaurenz, "If anybody can conjure up some hot isotopes, you should be able to do it."

"They have drums of the stuff down at Standart," said Alaurenz.

"How far is that?" asked Laurenz.

"About thirty miles," answered Alaurenz.

"Is it guarded?"

"Yes, but only on the periphery, because it's too dangerous for personnel to linger in the vicinity of the radiation," said Alaurenz. "If you can breach the wide area surrounding the waste dump, you will have free run of the facility. There are monitors, of course, and you would be seen in at least some of the activity. But the guards there would think only a couple of nuts would trespass there and would be captured when they tried to leave."

"And the nuttier we look, the less likely it is that the guards would rush to intervene," said Christian.

"Without doubt," said Alaurenz, envisioning the scene and now laughing at the whole idea. "They would probably monitor your escape but delay pursuit after they discovered the toxic nature of your booty. They will be in a general state of confusion created by the mere idea that anyone would do such a thing. By the time they got it together and coordinated with the Guardian police, it would be too late."

"Okay, the next thing is: how can you get the stuff in or on top of the Guardian headquarters to let it do its work?" asked Alaurenz.

"It may be easiest to just crash it into the entrance," said Laurenz. "I can use the same vehicle I will use to invade the hot repository in the first place. If we planted a small explosive under an open keg of the stuff, it would scatter all over the place. I should do this alone, because there's no sense in us both having to jettison our contaminated holos."

"Is this the only truck Alaurenz could find?" asked Christian as they inspected the vehicle. "It's a box truck."

"We're lucky it's not a semi," said Laurenz. "But it's got a manual shift, and it will take some getting used to."

"I hope you get the hang of it before your holo gets whiplash," said Christian. "As far as the truck goes, it will at least give you some extra heft when you crash the security at Standart and, if you make it, the entranceway to the Guardian headquarters. I will disengage and when I figure you have finished the task. Whatever the outcome, I will see you back on Earth."

"Let's hope it works. Here goes," said Laurenz.

The truck lurched a few times, traveled several yards, and lurched again when Laurenz shifted gears. As it disappeared out of sight, the reluctant truck seemed to have settled its score with the novice driver and now moved steadily away.

After a half hour's travel, Laurenz thought, *I'm just about there if my intuitive odometer serves me. The settled portions seem to be thinning out. Figures, I wouldn't want to live near such a facility either.*

Laurenz gunned the truck as he approached the guard house. The guards scattered when it was determined that the truck was not about to stop. Crashing through the flimsy barrier serving as a temporary restraint to the routine transfers of the dangerous material, he continued full speed to the unmanned depot containing the drums of radioactive material. Bringing the truck to a standstill, he checked the Geiger counter Alaurenz had provided.

Wow, he thought. *The thing is chirping away at the upper limit. My real self would last about twelve hours in its presence, and none of it would be pleasant. Now, I'll just put it in the cab on the seat beside me. He rolled one of the drums to the passenger's side and with difficulty hoisted it up on the seat and secured it with some rope.*

He sighed and said to himself, "Here goes."

Turning the truck back toward Charlsted, he gunned it and again crashed back through the entrance gate to the wide-eyed astonishment of the guards and made for the city. As he approached, the sound of sirens pierced the air. A barricade of police cruisers blocked his way. Laurenz floored the accelerator and crashed through, sending them askew with dents and creases and at the same time mangling the truck's front end.

He zoomed past the only vaguely familiar buildings while both thinking and appending his thoughts, *Just a few more blocks, I think.* "There," he mouthed with relief as he sighted the Guardian headquarters still some blocks away looming above the adjacent buildings and still topped with the mangled remnants of the statue.

Approaching the building at full speed, he crashed into the entranceway, scattering the few random visitors and strollers unlucky enough to be there. He wrenched the truck door open and confronted a hodgepodge of startled Guardians and service personnel. In the background, alarms began to sound drawing the attention away from Laurenz and the battered truck. Laurenz joined the mass exodus as confusion reigned.

I must get rid of this hot body of mine before I do in some citizens. Now where is a dumpster? thought Laurenz as he hustled into the maze of nearby buildings, avoiding any occasional passersby.

"There," he voiced with relief as he paused at the mouth of an alleyway. Hopefully the workers will just scoop up the container and truck it off to the dump. "Here goes." He pried open the top and slipped in. *Yuck*, was this last thought before he disengaged.

"Well, that worked out okay," said Laurenz as he emerged from his chamber to be greeted by Christian and Marcia. "They won't be using the headquarter site anytime soon as a transmission site. Now, according to Alaurenz, some of the smaller towns get the becalming signal from the larger ones nearby. Any lingering clusters of becalmed citizens can be dealt with by those who have been freed. Hopefully, they will be in the majority. Let's all get some exercise, rest up, and transfer back tomorrow. By the way, where's Freda?"

"She stayed till the becalming signal was back up and left disgusted," said Christian. "She's resting now and waiting for the next development."

"Well she should be pleased. It just happened. What I did zapped it for good, at least in the capital of Charlsted," said Laurenz who had warmed to the eccentric Freda.

"All ready," asked Laurenz as the earthlings assembled to transfer yet again to the trouble-ridden world of Otherearth. "Okay then. Retire to your chambers, and we will find out what has happened."

Upon their arrival, they were greeted by jubilant Alaurenz. "The media is liberated, and the chatter indicates that the torpid populace is coming to life. It looks like our struggle is over. Community groups are forming, and leaders are emerging from which politicos can emerge. Aside from an occasional diehard, the Guardians will hesitate to use the superior weaponry, because they know it will fail in the end and leave them at the mercy of a vengeful populace. What about Ganderk? We have him captive. Can we just let him loose to pursue his mischief?"

"I suggest you keep him at the lab until the situation has stabilized," said Laurenz. "Then you can let him loose to pursue whatever frustrated efforts he chooses. My sense is that the renewed awareness of the populace will never let either the clergy or a secret police gain the upper hand again. Unfortunately, he now knows where the lab is, so you will have to relocate again if you wish to have the backup of its troubleshooting potential.

"For our part, we will release to our world the astounding facts concerning our interaction and strive for a rational way forward. We cautiously believe that the physical and dimensional barriers that separate us should eliminate any bright ideas any either of our worlds might have for aggression or conquest."

POSTSCRIPT

Christian stood staring at Janize. She stared back with glistening eyes. Neither spoke, knowing that without the larger issues making the interworld contact imperative, their intimate bonding would end. Already aware that a real-life consummation of their intimacy would never happen, they were content with a proxy for it.

"Whatever excuse there is to revisit your world, I will try to be a part of it," said Christian. "In the meantime, you must get on with your life here. Hopefully, you will meet someone with as much affection for you as I have."

Janize nodded, unable to hold back tears.